SOMEONE HAS TO PAY

CLIFFORD MORRIS

Publishing Coordinator – Sharon Kizziah-Holmes

Paperback-Press
an imprint of A & S Publishing
A & S Holmes, Inc.

ISBN -13: 978-1-951772-02-4

ACKNOWLEDGMENTS

I would like to give special thanks to Nancy Chase, Jeff Ehrlich, Fred Hedgecoke, Allyn Collins and David Kendall for their invaluable comments and suggestions in the development and completion of this story.

Free People will Not be Economically Equal,
and economically equal people will not be free.
Lawrence Reed

CHAPTER ONE

$

THE STREET WAS QUIET AND ABANDONED. Dew glistened on recently mowed lawns. A rising glow in the east slowly vanquished the darkness. Neither a newspaper boy nor early morning jogger was in sight. No house dogs courageously yapping from behind protected fences.

Cleet Dixon sat at the kitchen table, stirring his coffee. Thick stubble blackened his face, a shock of chest hair exploded through the opening of his bathrobe. His heavy brow concealed a mind deep in thought. These were not the best days of his life.

Two sharp raps came at the front door, followed by a brief pause, then two more quick raps. It was just past six. Cleet pulled back the curtain enough to see a lone figure standing on the front steps. He unlocked the door and came face to face, once again, with a representative of his financial nightmare.

"Michael Cranfield, Mr. Dixon, Internal Revenue Service. I need to speak with you."

"What? At this hour?"

"I'll explain everything. May I come in?"

"What do you want?"

"We have to talk."

Cleet scowled and moved aside. Cranfield stepped into the house followed by two other men Cleet had not seen when he looked through the window. Another man named Edwards pulled a document from inside his suit jacket and stepped toward Dixon.

"I'm a duly sworn Revenue Officer of the United States Government. Both I, and these Special Agents, are here under authority of the U.S. Treasury to take possession of your personal property on this list not exempt by law. Such property is to be administratively seized to partially satisfy delinquent taxes owned by you to the federal treasury," Edwards said.

"Wha . . . What?" Cleet stammered. "You've got to be kidding."

"It's not a joke, and you know it. You've received numerous notices making you fully aware of this inevitability. A *Final Notice of Intent to Levy* and *Notice of Your Right to a Hearing* were issued and sent certified mail more than thirty days ago, as required by law. You made no effort to respond.."

"I've been making payments."

"Not according to your previously signed

agreement. You haven't cooperated with the Service to pay your delinquent tax, and your options to handle this obligation on your own accord are exhausted. The United States Treasury expects its money now."

"Is that why you brought your goons with you?"

Special Agent Frank Masters stepped forward and stared at Dixon until the homeowner blinked. Frank pulled back his jacket until the unmistakable butt of a pistol was visible."Just doing our job, sir."

The Dixon file was Edward's case. As a revenue officer it was his job to personally collect taxes owed and administratively seize personal property when necessary. The other two men with him, Michael Cranfield and Franks Masters, were Special Agents, authorized to carry weapons. They came along in case polite conversation didn't get the job done. Edwards withdrew an itemized list from his pocket and handed it to Cleet. "These items, I believe, are here at your residence."

Cleet glanced over the list. He couldn't get his eyes to focus.

"Daddy, what is it?"

A sleepy female voice pulled four sets of eyes toward the hallway.

"Nothing—nothing, go back to bed." Cleet returned his attention to the list.

"Who are these men?" A young woman wrapped in a pink terrycloth robe peered into the living room. The attention of the agents lingered an extra second in her direction.

"These men are from the IRS," Cleet said. "They found it necessary to come at the crack of dawn."

He looked up from his reading. "Did you expect us to be going somewhere?"

"We have the authority to seize the items shown, Mr. Dixon," Edwards said. "You'll have at least ten days to pay your back taxes and penalties before any of the items are auctioned."

"Like hell, you will!" Cleet's third-generation, twelve-gauge shotgun was listed. His father had hunted with that gun as a boy. The list included his liberty head dime collection, his extensive set of power tools, his wife's jewelry, an antique silver place setting for eight, all the fine china, the piano, and the motorboat.

"Mr. Dixon, don't make this harder on yourself than it has to be," Special Agent Michael Cranfield interjected. He had been standing quietly with Frank Masters near the front door, but decided it was time to serve the taxpayer a dose of reality. Michael stepped in front of Edwards. The whining would get Dixon nowhere, and the agents had other taxpayers to "visit" before the day was over.

"You can't just take my property. I've been paying you bloodsuckers what I can when I can."

"Sorry, but your time is up," Michael said.

"Sorry, my ass. Becky, get my lawyer on the phone." The young woman walked toward the house phone in the kitchen.

"We're not waiting on your lawyer," Michael replied. "A delivery truck will be here soon to load the items on that list. Besides, your lawyer would tell you what we're telling you."

"Go to hell. Why don't you get real jobs?" Cleet stepped toward Michael. "Do you believe anyone benefits when you run businesses and families into the ground?"

"Look, Dixon, the government has a legitimate claim to taxes assessed on your business profits, and you know it. You haven't paid. Time's up. Finito. Period. End of story. A seizure has been ordered on your personal property to help pay the delinquent taxes."

"I'm calling the police."

"You do that."

"Oh, I'm not calling them to help me. I know you've got them in your hip pocket. I'm calling the fire department, too. I want the whole damn neighborhood to see how you bastards conduct business." Cleet waved his arms in the air like a man so unjustly accused it was beyond all reason the plight he was forced to endure. "I bet you don't want a bunch of negative publicity, do you? That's why you showed up on my doorstep at dawn, isn't it?"

Michael was in a testy mood this particular morning. He'd had another spat with his wife and he hadn't slept well. But he saw his harsh approach was getting the taxpayer worked up. He tried to dial back the confrontation. "Okay, sir. Take it easy. Where are the listed items?"

"I'm not giving you anything." Cleet whipped himself into a self-righteous frenzy.

Michael nodded at Frank and Edwards, then walked into the kitchen.

"Sit down, Mr. Dixon," Frank said. But Cleet remained standing in the middle of the living room, his huge bulk covered in a flimsy robe, his eyes wide on the verge of tears.

Michael moved near the young woman. She was ready to punch numbers into the phone. "You don't want this to become any more difficult than it has to be, do you?"He spoke slowly and extended his hand for the phone. His gaze made contact with her wide, frightened eyes that searched his face for clues to his intentions.

"Get the hell out of there!" Cleet grabbed a heavy ashtray and hurled it at the doorway. It smashed against the wall and showered the kitchen doorway with shards of glass. Cleet dashed into the room oblivious to the broken glass he stepped on that cut his bare feet. He knocked Michael into the cupboards below the far counter, then yanked a butcher knife from a block of wood near the sink.

"Daddy, NO!" Becky cried.

The familiar voice made Cleet pause. Michael ran out the doorway into the dining room. Cleet threw the knife that twanged harmlessly off the door frame. Cleet grabbed a wooden rolling pin and sprang out the other kitchen door. A second later he was back in front of Michael. Cleet held the rolling pin high over his head. Michael drew his .38 revolver from the holster on his hip.

"Drop it, Dixon."

Panting hard and deep, Cleet took one, two, three strides toward Michael swinging the rolling pin with enough force to crack ribs and crush skulls.

A boom inside the confined walls of the house stabbed everyone's eardrums. The stench of sulfur drifted in a smoky haze. Cleet dropped to a knee. Michael stood stiffly against the wall, his arms hung limply, the gun dangled, held by two fingers.

And then came the sickening sound of something falling like a sack of potatoes bounding down the staircase. Everyone remained frozen as the sharp sound of the gunshot and the smoke cleared.

Becky screamed. Cleet was the first to reach the bleeding boy at the foot of the stairs. Lance Dixon groaned, his face contorted in pain. A circle of red began to stain his pajamas near his left hip.

"Good God," Cleet choked. "Please—someone call an ambulance."

CHAPTER TWO

$

EVERYONE FROZE AT THE SIGHT of the blood covered boy at the base of the stairs. Never before had Michael fired his service revolver in conducting his official duties. He returned his handgun to his holster with pained deliberation as if placing a favorite pet into a shallow grave and vaguely heard Frank on the phone calling an ambulance. Michael approached the groaning boy and frantic father. Michael watched as Cleet grabbed an arm cover from the couch, placed it over the boy's hip, and tied off the wound with the cloth belt from his robe.

The EMS team was soon at the door with the uniformed police right behind them. Michael, Frank, and Edwards had their badges out as two cops pulled them aside.

"You're going to have to wait here until a detective arrives," said one of the officers.

In the five years, Michael had worked with Frank, he had adopted Frank's cold, by-the-book approach when answering questions from the public, including cops. As Special Agents, he and Frank represented the nation's tax authority, authorized no less by the United States Treasury, Congress, and the 16th Amendment to the Constitution. They might get raked over the coals inside the Service for infractions here and there, but to the public, they were gods.

But he'd just shot a kid who couldn't be more than fifteen. Michael felt terrible though he dare not show it. He couldn't lose this job. It was this taxpayer's word against him, and the shot fired was justifiable. Frank and Edwards would back him up.

Within minutes of the shooting, the neighborhood awakened to the wail of sirens. People pulled back curtains and shuffled across lawns in hastily donned robes. Police cruiser emergency lights pounded a strobe of reds and blues against the backdrop of early morning light, and the street filled with whispering onlookers.

When the EMS team had Lance on the gurney and out of the house, Becky jumped into the back of the ambulance. She knelt near the head of her wounded brother whose face remained contorted in pain. With the slam of a door and a horn blast, the ambulance rolled down the driveway and picked up speed as it rounded a corner and disappeared.

The emergency technician started an IV. Splinters of bone protruded through the skin around the blue-black hole that seeped sporadic drops of blood. Until they reached the hospital, none of them would know if the bullet had torn into his guts.

No sooner had the siren wails faded in the distance than two detectives in business suits came through the door. The lead man flipped out his badge to one of the uniformed cops without saying a word and walked to the stairs where Cleet sat plying his fingers through thinning hair, still lost in a battle of overwhelming emotion.

"They shot my boy."

The two men glanced at the blood on the steps, then walked to the kitchen. "I'm Detective Collins" He flipped out his badge again. "This is Detective Williams. So what happened here?"

"Unfortunate altercation, I'm afraid," Michael said. "We were here to carry out an IRS administrative seizure. The debtor didn't see it that way and began making threats and attacked me."

"Hmmm." Collins rubbed his chin. "We'll need the three of you to come to the station to make a statement.

"First we have to report to our office. Regulations," Michael said. "Here's my card. The boy should be at the hospital by now. The homeowner will probably have plenty to say, but I have witnesses. We never draw our weapons unless we have to."

With that, the IRS agents walked out, leaving the cops somewhat flatfooted. But they would meet again. Michael had bigger troubles to consider in the form of IRS Area Director, Everett Barnes.

Michael rode with Frank. Edwards left in his

own car.

"You did good with that detective," Frank said to Michael as they drove away. "Give'um the hardcore, no quarter routine and the public buys it lock, stock, and barrel. The cops, too. You handled it perfectly. In a few days, this will be nothing more than a passing memory."

"Yeah but . . . Frank. I don't feel good about this at all."

"Awe shit, Cranfield. Don't go getting weak in the knees now. You gotta be a hard ass with Barnes. Tell them there was no other way. You got cornered. The guy was threatening bodily harm. Just like you told the cop."

"I'll tell him it was an accident. It was, I didn't mean to fire it. I thought the guy would back off when he saw the gun."

"No, no, no. None of that. We don't have accidents. You say, let's see, it was a warning shot. You aimed the shot high on the wall to freeze him in his tracks. But when he swung at you, the shot went through the underside of the staircase and hit the kid sitting on the steps. Damn kid was probably sitting there the whole time listening to his father rant and fume, but you didn't know he was there."

"I hope he's all right," Michael said, eyes closed, kneading his temples, talking toward the dashboard.

"Christ all mighty, he was hit in the leg after the slug went through an inch or so of wood. The kid will be fine. Think about what else might have happened. The way the father was getting out of control in another ten seconds either you or I would have had to shoot the guy in the head."

They pulled into the parking garage of the Dallas Federal Building on Commerce Street. On the elevator ride to the IRS offices, Michael felt his chest constricting.

Barnes was waiting for them. He sat on the front edge of his desk and began to roll up his shirt sleeves as three men walked into his office. "Okay, talk to me."

"There's been a shooting," Michael said.

"I know that! What happened?"

"It's the Dixon file. The guy got all worked up, threatening, knocked me across the kitchen, and kept coming at me to beat my brains out."

"Okay, okay. Get to the gun, Cranfield. I don't have all day."

"I pulled the gun, but he didn't stop. So I fired a warning shot."

"What? We don't fire warning shots." Barnes slammed shut a half opened file drawer, then slammed shut the file drawer below it.

He threw an ashtray and a knife at me and started swinging a rolling pin as he came at me."

"Good grief, Cranfield. A rolling pin?"

Just the way the words came out sounded funny, and Frank cracked a slight smile even as he avoided Barnes' glare.

"And where were you in all of this?" Barnes turned to Edwards.

"I was right there, but it all happened so fast. Cranfield did the best he could without killing the guy."

"Yeah, but the bullet hit his kid. Is that right?" Barnes knew the answer to his question before he asked it, and he shook his head. Something like this had never happened on his watch before. How would he ever explain it to the brass upstairs? An incident like this created unwanted attention, made the Service come across as a bunch of rampaging thugs. Negative publicity cost the agency their ace in the hole—intimidation value. The only kind of attention the IRS wanted was the kind that made men quiver in their shoes, thankful that the audit had happened to the other guy, that someone else had had their bank account seized. Bad publicity incensed the public, made them uncooperative. If this incident made the headlines, it could haunt the Dallas office for months, and reduce timely collections by tens of thousands of dollars.

Barnes squeezed his chin and plied his beleaguered face with his meaty fingers. He walked to the narrow vertical rectangle that was his office window and peered out for a moment. Then he dropped into his chair and began making phone calls. Barnes called his supervisor, and they talked for ten minutes. He called the hospital, and lastly, the Dallas Morning News. He reached an assistant editor he knew on a first name basis and asked him to hold coverage of the incident until all the facts were in. Satisfied that immediate fires were extinguished, Barnes returned his focus to his three agents.

"Collections are way down, and now you go and pull this," Barnes said.

The call to the newspaper commanded center stage in Michael's mind. "You got the Morning News to hold the story?"

"Yeah, they'll hold it. They got no story yet, just bits and pieces. It'll give me time to write up a counter-scenario to your stunt. I'll make it read like you barely got out of there with your life and the taxpayer is being charged with assaulting a government agent." Barnes rubbed his chin again and exhaled a sigh of relief. "Whenever the paper runs the story, both sides will be in there. Maybe it won't look like you were a careless thug."

Frank nudged Michael to get off the subject."It's just like Michael said, Chief. The ole boy couldn't deal with reality and escalated the whole situation."

A rap came at Barnes' door, and a man walked in and displayed his badge. "I'm Detective Collins. I've already met your agents. They told me earlier that they needed to report to you before they came to the station and made statements. So now that they've reported, I need them to come with me."

"What kind of questions do you have, Detective?" Barnes asked.

"Someone got shot, specifically a citizen of Dallas, Texas. It's our standard procedure to take statements from everyone present," Collins replied, his head cocked, eyes locked into Barnes' gaze.

"Can't you ask your questions here?" Barnes stepped from behind his desk. "Look, Detective, these men are federal agents. We also conduct investigations into incidents like this, I assure you."

Collins turned and faced Michael. Collins appeared well past middle-age. His face was a portrait of sleepless nights, long stake-outs, and gruesome crime scenes. "You are aware, I'm sure, Mr. Cranfield, when you pull the trigger on a firearm, you are responsible for the direction the bullet travels and anything it hits." Collins paused to let the full weight of his statement soak in. Michael was fully aware of the implication.

"So if you were fighting it out with Mr. Dixon, how did you manage to shoot his boy on the other side of the room?" Collins prodded.

Barnes interjected himself in the conversation. "Detective, I'll have these men available to make statements, but not this morning. We need to speak with our legal counsel first. You understand, don't you."

"No, I don't understand. If these men have nothing to hide, why can't they make preliminary statements now?"

The three agents remained quiet, but Michael grew nervous. He had to keep this job. His wife detested what he did for a living but enjoyed the government benefits. This matter wouldn't result in criminal charges, would it? The department would have his back, wouldn't they? Or if the heat got too great would they simply provide a modicum of legal representation, then cut him loose to fend for himself?

"We're not done here," Collins said as he prepared to go. "Our department has questions about this incident, and we're going to get answers. In the meantime, we all live and work in the same town. If you don't mind using some restraint collecting money so desperately needed by the government, maybe your boys would let the next generation get old enough to pay taxes."

Michael saw Barnes' eyelids open a fraction, and

a cold stare focus on the detective. But Barnes held his tongue. He shut the office door, faced Michael, Frank, and Edwards and spoke the thoughts that had been grinding in his head from the moment he got word of the shooting.

"When I spoke to the hospital, they said the boy was still in surgery. If you had shot the taxpayer, we could explain everything away. If he died, it wouldn't be good, but at least we could have explained it away as justified. We could still have collected our levy. But now—you better hope and pray that kid recovers completely. If he dies or is permanently disabled, that file is wasted. If that boy dies, we'll never collect another dime."

CHAPTER THREE

$

THE AMBULANCE SCREECHED to a stop under the emergency room portico. An army of attendants surrounded Lance's gurney before it was even through the sliding glass doors. Becky found herself alone. She stepped from the back of the ambulance, cold in nothing but pajamas and a robe despite the pleasant morning. She pulled the robe tight to her throat. A dizzying swirl of events had transpired and she was confused as to what to do next. She jumped as the motion sensors on the hospital doors snapped open in front of her. The waiting room was all but vacant. An older gentleman slept with his chin on his chest, a magazine about to side from his lap. A young woman rocked a fussy, snot-nosed tot, if not to sleep at least to silence.

"I can help you over here," a woman beckoned from behind a glass window.

Still dazed and lost in thought, Becky sat in a flimsy, plastic chair with thin metal armrests.

"You came in with the patient in the ambulance?"

"Yes."

"I need to get some information. Name?"

"Lance Dixon."

"Relationship?"

"He's my brother."

"Insurance company?"

The questioning snapped Becky from her numbed thoughts. "I don't know. He got shot and might be dying in there. Can't this wait?"

"The doctors will do everything they can do. But I can't assign your brother a room until I know how this is going to be paid."

"Is that so?" Becky laughed a reflexive release of stress and frustration. But instantly, she realized she was half-naked in a public place with a hundred questions spinning in her head and no one to help her.

"Where are your parents?"

Becky threw up her hands. "I'm sure my father will be here soon. He was talking to the police."

"Okay, well let me have you fill this out while you're waiting. I'm sure we'll get word from the doctor's soon."

Becky stood and handed the clipboard back to the admissions clerk. "You fill it out. I've got to see my brother."

"Wait, you can't go back there."

Becky pushed her way through the emergency room door and saw Lance on an exam table as the blood-covered ambulance gurney whisked past her. Her ears caught bits of conversation, "full set of lower x-rays," "prepare OR #2," "transfusions," "someone help that young lady to the waiting room."

"LANCE."

"This way please, ma'am," a masked attendant gently took her arm.

"I want to see my brother. How is my brother?"

"He's doing fine." The words were spoken softly but sounded like hollow hogwash, a memorized response without any meaning. "I'll have someone come sit with you. The doctor will give you a full report as soon as possible."

Becky heard the door close behind them, the harsh light of the corridor pressed on her eyes as the medicinal odor of the hallway choked her nostrils. Two steps later, her head swooned, her knees gave way, and she fainted in a heap on the floor.

****

Cleet rushed into the hospital to the receptionist desk. "Lance Dixon." The woman was taken aback when she looked up. Cleet was the closest thing to a madman she'd ever seen. She pushed her chair back, ready to flee. He wore a blazer over a t-shirt, trousers, and slippers. His hair looked as if it had never seen a comb. His eyes blazed fear and desperation below a hairline beaded with sweat.

"Sir, may I . . ."

"Lance Dixon. He was brought to emergency an hour ago. Where is he?"

The woman checked the computer. "Follow the green line. They'll be able to . . ."

Cleet was off, zigzagging through the building. His path ended at a nurse's station.

"Lance Dixon," his words gushed forth, out of breath.

"Come with me," said a nurse.

Down another corridor through a huge oak door into a partitioned bedroom bathed in sunlight, Becky rested in a hospital bed near the window.

"I'll leave you two alone for now," said the nurse.

A perplexed look overtook Cleet's face as he stepped to the bedside. "What are you doing in here?"

"I fainted or something. I guess the ambulance ride was too much. I don't know. It all happened so fast."

"Lance. How is Lance?"

"They took him to surgery."

"And?"

"That's all I know. Once we got here, the hospital staff wouldn't let me see him."

"You haven't found out anything?"

"They wouldn't tell me. Until the surgery is complete, they may not have anything to say."

"Good god, is he even alive?"

"Yes, he's alive. Please don't yell at me."

"Where's the nurse. I want answers."

"Please wait here and sit down. I'm as worried as you are, but you know the doctors are doing all they can."

Cleet inhaled a deep breath and fell exhausted in the chair. "Why again are you in here?" he asked.

"I fainted in the hallway. They drew some blood and gave me some juice. I'm feeling better already. I think it was the stress. I called Matt. He's coming over." She reached out and touched her father's hand. "Are we in serious financial trouble, daddy?"

Cleet avoided her gaze. "Nothing I can't get us out of. You know what your mother always said, 'the sun shines with promise and starlight helps dreams grow.'"

For a moment, Becky could do nothing but remain silent and study the aging contours of her father's beleaguered face. "Daddy, mother is not with us anymore, and that's a childish saying to get babies to go to sleep. Lance and I aren't babies anymore. Tell me what's going on."

Cleet stood and clenched the rail at the foot of the bed. "Well, if I didn't care whether or not my employees had a decent benefits package or if your university wasn't squeezing me for every last nickel, among other things, I might be able to march to Uncle Sam's drum and pay them every damn cent they'd like to see. Everybody wants all they can get, and they wanted it yesterday. And now, that bastard comes in our house and shoots Lance." Cleet paced between the window and the door. "I'm going to make that son-of-a-bitch pay."

"Daddy, don't make it worse. Come here. Sit back down. Lance will be all right."

A young man wearing a long-sleeved, striped soccer jersey came through the door. "Hi, Mr. D."

He brushed back a shock of brown hair and leaned over the bed and kissed Becky. "How are you feeling?"

"Better."

"Any word on Lance?"

"We're still waiting."

The huge oak door opened again, and a Candy Striper entered in her red and white dress. She had the bounce and exuberance of a teenager with a beaming smile to match. Her body language spoke of a new volunteer ready and willing to brighten every patient's day and make each of them her friend. "Well, we now know why you felt faint ma'am." She stepped to the foot of the bed to address them all. "You're pregnant. Congratulations."

A palpable silence enveloped the room and within seconds the young volunteer realized she was the only one smiling.

"What?" Cleet jumped from the chair. Utter incredulity and inner pain etched in that single sound. "Pregnant? You two can't keep your hands off each other."

"Daddy, we're going to get married," Becky pleaded.

"Oh my," muttered the girl as she backed from the room. "I'm so sorry."

"But you're not married, are you?" Cleet's neck and face flushed red; blood vessels bulged under his skin. "Is this what I'm spending my hard earned money for? So you can sleep around campus with every smiling jock with a clever line?"

"Don't say that. It's not like that at all," Becky

said.

"Mr. D, wait a minute," Matt stuttered.

"Keep your damn mouth shut, college boy. On the very day, my son gets shot. I'm thankful your mother isn't around to hear this. Just how ungrateful and stupid can you be, Rebecca? I thought you had goals? How can you do that now? How are you going to pursue a career raising a baby? You're not even halfway to your degree. You expect this bright-eyed yokel to take care of you?"

"Mr. Dixon, I love Becky. We'll take care of this."

"Yeah, right. Get out of my way. All I can think of is how this would have broken your mother's heart. I'm going to see what I can find out about your brother."

When the door closed, Matt stepped to the bed, leaned down, and embraced Becky.

"Oh, Matt, I know he didn't mean what he said, but it still hurts."

"It'll be all right, Baby. I can get the money to pay for it. It won't interrupt your classes or nothing."

"What are you talking about? Pay for what?"

"You know, it's done every day. It's a simple procedure, and we can move on with the rest of our lives."

"You want me to have an abortion? Is that what you're trying to say?"

"Well yeah. We've got lots of time. We'll have a whole houseful of kids, I promise."

Becky choked back a laugh. "You say you love me, yet you want me to kill our first child? Doesn't something about that sound wrong to you?"

"Becky, we're too young. Your dad's right. We don't need to be trying to raise a child right now."

"So you want me to kill it? You didn't mind seducing me, but now that I'm pregnant you want to get rid of the inconvenience by flushing it down the toilet. Is that it?"

"You're upset."

"You're damn right I'm upset. I've been upset all morning. But that doesn't mean I've lost my mind. I will not kill my first baby or my second baby or any baby because I might have to rearrange my schedule." She turned away from him.

"I'll wait if you want me to. I'll give you a ride home."

Becky shook her head. "I think I'll rest here a little longer. I want to be here when Lance gets out of surgery."

"I love you, Becky."

She closed her eyes and put her head on the pillow. After Matt left the room, she raised herself on her elbow and looked outside at several robins fluttering around a thick, branched-out elm, and the view began to blur as though rainwater was running down the window.

CHAPTER FOUR

$

IT WAS PAST ELEVEN when Barnes dismissed Michael and Frank from his office. Revenue Officer Edwards had left some time ago. He didn't carry a weapon. Edward's version of events at the Dixon home would be required by investigators, but concerning the discharge of a firearm, he was out of the picture.

With Barnes' outbursts and Detective Collin's not-so-subtle hints concerning his possible criminal culpability, Michael wanted nothing more than to lie in a dark room with a cold drink and forget about the morning. Mentally he was exhausted, guilt-ridden, beside himself with second-guesses and remorse. Michael had tried to browbeat a taxpayer into acquiescence concerning his tax liability only to be confronted by an irrational man ready to do him bodily harm. Michael followed Frank to the parking garage.

"I'll take this next one," Frank said. "Just back me up. I've talked to this ole boy before. To look at him, you'd think he was some poor, down-on-his-luck sharecropper doing the best he can knocking out a few pieces of furniture in a wood shop. But I know better. We're going to make this a date he'll remember."

Michael rubbed the bridge of his nose. "Where are we going?" he asked.

"The Beasley file, cabinet building wood shop. Service's been sending this guy notices for a year and a half, enough to wallpaper a barn."

"Oh yeah," Michael said, "thanks for the 'warning shot' alibi. Barnes really took to that."

"Sorry," Frank replied. "It was all that crossed my mind at the time, but it was a damn site better than telling Barnes the shooting was an accident."

The men drove down Industrial Avenue behind a semi-tractor dealership to a metal building about 30' X 50'. The smell of freshly cut wood shavings hit them as soon as they entered the building. Sawdust piles stood under most machines as the high-pitched whine of buzz saws filled the building. Frank tapped a gray-haired man on the shoulder. The man turned and removed his goggles.

"Special Agent Masters IRS, Mr. Beasley." Frank delivered the standard spiel. A lathe turned off. One by one, saws quit humming. The building grew quiet.

Beasley wiped his forehead with his sleeve and appeared not to have heard what Frank said.

Frank handed Beasley the paperwork. "If you don't have the full amount to pay your back taxes, we're here to lock the business up."

"Well... well, we got a couple of jobs in the back ready to be delivered," Beasley said.

"Set them outside and ship them out. That's the best I can do," Frank said.

"How much does it say I owe?"

"Look for yourself." The man opened to the first page. Frank pointed to the figure. "$64,644."

"That much, still? I've been paying extra every month. It's got to be more penalties and fees. You people don't want me to get out of the hole."

"All I can say, sir, is you're shut down until the taxes are paid. The government is entitled to a percentage of your business profits. You know that. These assessments have to be collected promptly, and this delinquency has been on the books for some time. The Service has tried to work with you."

Beasley now appeared bewildered and looked around the building. "But I have seven other men who count on this shop for their living. We can't just stop what we're doing."

"Yes, you can, and you're required to do so. Turn off the lights and any equipment you have running. I'm going to padlock all doors with a sign by each one. Anyone who enters the building while the signs are posted is committing a felony." Frank announced what was to occur with no more inflection in his voice than a song leader telling a congregation which page to turn to in their hymnals.

"How can I pay you if I can't work?"

"Mr. Beasley, please read the entire document.

At this point, your options are few, but you can still work with the Service to get this matter resolved."

"But I can't pay what you say I owe unless I work."

"The Service may decide to sell the building."

"I don't own the building."

"Then they may sell your tools and machines to pay the tax."

"My machines are worth much more than what you say I owe."

"Fine," Frank said, without any empathy in his voice. "You'll receive the difference in the form of a check if the equipment sells for more than you owe."

Michael closed his eyes and mentally shook his head. He knew at a government fire-sale auction all of the lathes, saws, planes, routers and expensive hand tools would be lucky to sell for twenty cents on the dollar. Beasley would never receive money back. He would still have a tax bill to pay. For the first time in his government career, Michael felt empathy for a delinquent taxpayer.

Beasley's body posture visibly fell. Beasley ushered his men to the back of the building while Frank went to the car for padlocks and signs. What Michael witnessed was nothing new. He and Frank had conducted numerous business closures. But today, a hollow emptiness gnawed in Michael's gut as he watched Beasley and his men move a desk and several cabinet assemblies into the yard, then watch dumbstruck as the overhead door was closed and locked from the inside.

The procedure was so routine --- until today.

Michael had never even remotely considered the impact their work had on the individuals involved. It wasn't personal; it was his job. But today, an awareness he had never felt before rumbled inside his chest. His thoughts were conflicted. His reasoning and his feelings were at odds and he felt vaguely ill. He had to get his mind off the old man who ran the wood shop. Some distasteful things in life simply had to be done. "Let's go get something to eat," he said to Frank as they returned to the car.

Frank and Michael headed for lunch at Calientes on North Greenville and took a corner table.

"I can't get the kid out of my mind," Michael said as they waited on their food. "You know, I've got two girls. The last thing I wanted to do was injure someone to collect revenue."

"Keep it down," Frank said. "The walls have ears."

"What am I going to do? Jan will kill me if I lose this job. She's going to kill me anyway when she finds out what happened."

"Tell her straight up. Get it out in the open," Frank said. "If she doesn't jump to a bunch of unfounded conclusions and go through a gamut of histrionics like the women in my life, you'll be on top of it. You're going to have to suck it up for a while. Give it some time."

"She'll think it was all my fault even before I get the whole story out. Her mind works that way."

"Listen—it happened to me once," Frank said. "Nine years ago, before you were around, a biker wannabe leveled a sawed-off shotgun at me. I shot him in the chest right in front of his wife and kids.

He died right there on his lawn.

"The Service conducted its investigation. I spent a month playing gopher for that pack of pasty-faced auditors on the fifth floor. The shooting was declared justifiable. Hey, there's a price to pay for firing your weapon, but that doesn't mean I'd hesitate to use it again to protect myself or my partner."

Their drinks and Mexican entrees arrived, and they sat quietly. Frank inhaled his enchiladas as though he hadn't eaten in a week while Michael picked at his food. "Yeah, but he's just a kid," Michael said almost to himself. He sipped his drink. Margaritas gave him heartburn, but he loved them anyway.

"I need to go to the firing range," Frank said. "I've got less than a week to get re-qualified. When are you due?"

"About a month, I think," Michael said. "I'll go with you. Might as well get it out of the way."

The men finished lunch and headed for an indoor range in Garland. The Service had arrangements with a number of private ranges where agents could practice and get qualified without dealing with the oppressive heat of the Service's outdoor range in Oak Cliff.

Standard issue was the Tauras .38 caliber revolver that held five rounds. Against a long rifle the gun was as useful as a pee-shooter against a Sherman tank. But in confined space at close range it could blow a hole through a two-hundred pound man. More than anything, the guns gave stark evidence that the jig was up. When Special Agents of the Internal Revenue Service were on the scene a taxpayer's days of bull shit and delay were over.

Their usual assignments were investigations of organized crime, tax fraud cases, and tax evasion schemes. Michael and Frank accompanied Edwards on some of his administrative seizures because the Dallas Police Department had declined to make officers available in recent years.

Michael and Frank showed their badges and signed in. After a warm-up, a range observer had to witness and sign off that each agent fired five consecutive rounds at twenty-five feet into the target's first inner circle next to the bull's eye. Each shot was separate and apart from the previous shot. Next, each man had to rapid fire five rounds into another target no wider than the second inner circle. Passing the second phase was critical. The test required handling the gun's recoil and getting the weapon quickly back on target.

Three attempts were allowed. Both men accomplished the tasks in their first attempt. After qualifying, they continued to practice for another half hour.

When they left the range it was half past three. They could go back downtown and shuffle paper until five or they could call it a day.

"Listen," Frank said. "I know just the place to get your mind off this morning. I'll buy you a drink and we can get out of this heat."

Frank drove to a gentleman's club on Greenville Avenue, a place called Sugar's. As soon as he passed through the lobby, Michael stepped into a different world. Pulsating colored lights flickered to rapid dance music that reverberated off the walls. Elevated stages displayed gyrating, top-less female perfection. Instantly, Michael forgot the noise of the traffic and the heat of the day. For the moment, he forgot about work and the shooting of Lance Dixon.

Frank found a table and ordered drinks. "Relaxing and easy on the eye, wouldn't you say?" Frank said as he leaned across the table and smiled.

"I'm married," Michael said.

"Yeah, but it's all show. All looky, no touchy. Last time I checked, looking don't constitute adultery. If you want to be friendly, a wad of one-dollar bills will last a long time. As long as you've got green paper in your hands, the girls will answer your every beck and call."

"How often do you come in here?"

"As often as I can. See that little sweetie up there? Frank pointed. "That's Misty. Cute thing, huh? Wait till you see the headlights she's hiding under that gauzy pink chiffon."

Michael took a hefty drink of his fresh margarita. "Maybe I should head home. I can call a cab."

"Oh no," Frank protested. "The day is young. There's someone I want you to meet. Real friendly and easy on the eye. Name's Elaine. She's got the sympathetic ear of Mother Theresa, and she'll melt your troubles away. Really, she's a sweetheart. You gotta let me introduce you."

"I don't need to be telling my troubles to no stripper."

"Don't tell her nothing. I'm just talking about getting out of your routine, loosen up, get your mind on something else." Frank jumped up, moved to the aisle as a dancer headed for a side stage. He whispered in her ear, and returned to the table. "That's Elaine. I asked her to come over after she finished her routine."

Michael gazed at the brightly lit stage and tried to focus. What he saw gave him the incentive to concentrate. Fully dressed at the outset, Elaine took her time disrobing as the music grew in volume and her garments fell away, revealing long legs and copper-golden skin. At the end of the performance, she was clad in all of a scanty swatch of pink cloth that posed as panties over a black G-string, and a garter on each thigh to hold her tips. When Elaine danced the cash rolled in, and her thighs appeared wrapped in green wreaths. After a brief stop to dry off and redress, Elaine stopped at their table.

"You look gorgeous, as always," Frank said, as he stood and adjusted her chair. "This is Michael. We had some extra time. Thought we'd get out of the heat for a while.

"Glad you did. Nice to meet you, Michael. I'm Elaine."

"Can I buy you a drink?" was all Michael could think to say, but his thoughts had shifted into overdrive. She was beautiful, probably mid-twenties with an easy smile and brilliant eyes. In the semi-darkness, he couldn't determine their color, but it hardly seemed to matter. She was gracious and professional, not fawning or pandering as he had assumed most strippers would be.

"Sure, I'll have a gin and tonic."

"I'll be back shortly," Frank said

She settled into a chair beside Michael as Frank

disappeared into the darkness. "Known Frank long?"

"Couple of years."

"He's mysterious in a way, but a nice guy at heart. Likes to loosen his tie a bit if you know what I mean?"

"Yeah, that's Frank," Michael replied, as a waitress in tight red shorts and long, white leather boots stopped to take their order. She wore a skimpy white blouse, the shirt tails tied in a knot above her navel.

"How about you?" Elaine asked. "I bet you get enough pressure in your nine to five. That's what Sugar's is all about—relieving stress." She smiled again in an open, friendly way. "What kind of work do you do, Michael?"

"My work is routine. Not much to tell."

"You're a businessman. You own your own business. I can tell by the way you act."

"I wish, but that's not the case. It's quite routine."

He would not tell her the truth about his job no matter how many times she asked. He learned early on that revealing his occupation brought one of two reactions in people—both bad. They either got that distant look in their eyes as though he were a leper or they began asking tax questions plying him for information. Both reactions made him bitter. If he wanted to have a casual conversation, he had to remain mum about his work.

She probably wanted to get an idea as to how much he was worth. He wanted to change the subject. "Oh well, work is work. We all have some stress to deal with, don't we?"

Elaine nodded. "But I can help you relieve all that."

"Thanks, but no. I don't know what you have in mind, but I'm married."

Elaine's eyes brightened, and she cocked her head. "Oh, most of the men here are married. They go home to their wives and kids every evening. Sugar's a break from the daily grind, like I said, a little harmless entertainment from me to you. Frank already paid for it. He wants you to have a good time. Let's go to the back where we can have our own little table."

Michael followed her behind a thick velvet curtain, and took a seat at a small round table with a single spotlight shining from above.

Elaine stood in front of him, gyrated to the music, and stroked her body. She threw her head back and her chest forward and eased onto his lap. Michael's last feeble effort of protest caught in his throat, and he leaned back in his chair. She rubbed her crotch up and down his thigh. Her breasts grazed his chin. Michael's senses nestled into the tactile connection. Then Elaine's body jerked.

Her voice stammered. "I know some things get hard when I dance, but it's not there."

Michael's thoughts drifted for a second longer, then slammed into his brain as her odd statement made sense. She had touched the butt of his pistol. He had forgotten to leave it in the car.

"Ah, jeez." Michael helped her from his lap and jumped to his feet. "I got a permit. I didn't mean to bring it in here."

"It's okay, baby. I'm quiet. Lots of people carry

heat in Texas," after a pause, she added,

"but not people with boring jobs."

"Yeah—here's a twenty. I got to go."

"Come back soon, Michael. I like you." Elaine smiled and straightened her skimpy attire as she stuffed the bill in her bra.

CHAPTER FIVE

$

CLEET SPENT THE NIGHT beside Lance's hospital bed. Sleep came in fitful spurts no more than twenty minutes at a time. He could not relax; his mind would not rest. He sat in silence as the morning nurse checked the IV running into Lance's forearm and the electrodes attached to his chest. Next, she checked the monitors next to his bed. Cleet was hungry but didn't have the motivation to walk down the hall and buy so much as a candy bar. He closed his eyes and rested his head on the back of the chair,

When the sun was well up, Becky walked into the room, smartly dressed, ready to attend classes. She walked to the bed and brushed Lance's hair off his forehead, then turned and faced her father. "Did he sleep well?"

Cleet backhanded the air as if swatting a fly. "I guess he slept well. He's been like that all night. Nobody tells me anything. I have no idea how long he'll be this way."

"Daddy, I'm so sorry about yesterday. I didn't know I was pregnant. I would have told you if I'd known."

"It hardly matters how I found out, Rebecca," her father's voice laced with disappointment and condescension. "I thought you had more sense."

"We're going to get married."

"Yeah, whatever" Cleet was out of the chair, his voice rising. "But let me tell you a few things right now. You better get married, 'cause you're not raising any kid in my house as a single parent. And if you decide to get rid of it, don't come looking to me for abortion money."

"Good grief, Matt said that, too. Is that the way men think? For an unplanned pregnancy, you just get rid of it?—throw it out like a used box? I don't want an abortion."

"Is that what he said?" Cleet glared at her.

"Yes."

"That's what I thought, a real honorable guy. Dump him. He's just out to have a good time."

"I want to have the baby, daddy."

"Okay, have the baby. If soccer jock is still around—get married, but it's going to interrupt your studies. If he's long gone, you can put it up for adoption."

"You're not listening," she said. "I want my baby."

"Rebecca, use your head."

"I am. I want this baby even if I have to raise it by myself."

"Then you can kiss college goodbye. Plan right now to get a job. You want it, you support it. I've got more on my mind than I can handle right now, and I'm not about to help raise a bastard child."

Becky could only swallow and shake her head. "Why have you gotten this way?"

"I could ask you the same thing. You think everything flows your way just because you're pretty. It's high time to grow up, Rebecca."

She sighed. "I'm going to classes now. You can call me when Lance wakes up if you want to." She placed her hand on her brother's cheek and stood beside the bed for several minutes. Then, she turned and left the room without saying another word.

A short time later, a familiar face pushed through the door and reintroduced himself to Cleet. It was the police detective he had spoken to yesterday at the house.

"How's your boy doing, Mr. Dixon?"

"He's still sedated. The doctors said the bullet hit his pelvis, and they removed fragments of bone. They won't comment yet on his long term prospects."

"I'm pulling for him. I'm sure many people are." Detective Collins walked to the window and surveyed the view from the second floor. "I figured I'd find you here. I talked to the agents involved and their supervisor. I intended to interview your daughter and this young man as soon as he was well enough to answer questions." Detective Collins turned and faced Dixon. "But—this morning I got a call from the DA's office to close our investigation."

"What?" Cleet gripped the foot of the bed with both hands.

"The Feds are conducting their own investigation into the matter."

"They can't do that. You can't let them. One of their agents shot my boy, and they're going to do their own investigation? You know that ain't right. They want your department out of the picture so they can cover it up."

"I can't comment about that, Mr. Dixon. I just thought you should know."

"They shot my boy."

"Take it easy and sit down. I intend to ask around on my own. I have questions I want answered, but I can't do anything more in an official capacity."

Cleet refused to sit, and his voice rose. "You've got to make them accountable for what they did, detective."

"They said you provoked the incident."

"Like hell, I did. Those agents were looking for an excuse to fire their guns."

"What do you mean by that?"

"Oh, hell." Cleet pulled at his hair. "I can't think straight. Look at him. I couldn't sleep all night. You can't let them get away with a slap on the wrist."

"Like I said, I'm going to do some checking around on my own time. But you need to get some rest. Really. There's nothing you can do right now. Why don't you go home and try to get a few hours of sleep?"

"Maybe . . . maybe."

As soon as Collins left, Cleet was at the nurses' station asking to be called as soon as his son was conscious. He needed time away from the medicinal smelling tomb they called a hospital, but a few hours of sleep were not among his priorities.

He drove to the office. He pulled himself from behind the steering wheel and gazed at the faded black letters on the building: Dixon Metal Fabricators. His executive secretary, Dorothy, scooted from behind her desk the moment he entered and followed him to his office.

"We're all so sorry to hear . . ."

He cut her off with a wave of his hand. "Have a seat. I want you to coordinate with Simpson and make sure all of our finished orders are shipped as soon as possible. Then I want all of the accounts receivable over thirty days old called and harassed until they pay their damn bills."

Dorothy sank into her chair. "Is there anything else I can do?"

"No, that's all," Cleet said. "I'll be away from the office for several days. Any questions?"

Dorothy shook her head. The moment she left Cleet's office the phone rang.

"Mr. Dixon, my name is Everett Barnes. I know you have a lot on your mind today, but it's important I speak with you for a few minutes."

"Okay, what can I do for you?"

"I'm the Dallas Regional IRS Supervisor."

Cleet sat up straight in his chair.

"I want you to know how truly saddened we all are at yesterday's unfortunate incident."

At that instant, Cleet was dumbstruck. He couldn't utter a peep. His tongue was dry as shoe leather; the telephone felt as heavy as an anvil in his grip.

"The entire situation is being thoroughly investigated. We want your explanation of events. You'll have plenty of time to tell your side of the story. I work for the government, everyone's government. We have to collect legitimate taxes, but we never condone overly aggressive methods that endanger the public."

"You're a damn liar. All you want is a nice clean cover up to get the heat off your ass, and get business back to usual."

"Mr. Dixon, everyone is sorry about what happened. As for the investigation, everything I said is true."

"Sorry . . . Sorry. That doesn't do a thing for my boy. He got shot. What if he's paralyzed? What if he never walks again?"

"I wish the best for your son. I want you to have my direct telephone number. Call me if you have any questions, or for any reason." Barnes gave Cleet the number to his private line, then said goodbye.

Cleet sat at his desk in a daze. A plan of action was forming in his mind. He wasn't taking the violent home intrusion lying down. The phone call from the bureaucratic asshole wasn't appreciated, and he knew the condolences were less than sincere. He regained his composure and considered his options. He couldn't bring down an entire federal department on his own, but the target he wanted had a name. He would focus his energy and resources on the single object of his contempt, and make him suffer an even greater measure of anguish than had been dealt to him.

He felt better now that he'd made a decision. He would become the man's shadow and exact revenge on him and his family. He was about to make life a living hell for IRS Special Agent Michael Cranfield.

CHAPTER SIX

$

ICHAEL LEFT SUGARS embarrassed, ashamed, mostly irritated. He took a cab back to the office to get his car. Then he meandered north on side streets until he was forced onto Preston Road to cross over LBJ Freeway. It was dark when he got home.

A leftover supper sat in the refrigerator in a Tupperware bowl. He dished out a concoction of spaghetti and meatballs, popped it in the microwave, and grabbed a slice of bread to add to his gourmet meal. He supposed the girls were in their room. He tapped on the door. Tonya cracked it open.

"I'm home. You want some more supper?"

"We're full. We ate already."

"Want some help with your homework?"

"We're done. We got a new CD."

"Okay, I wanted you to know I was here." The door closed in his face before he finished speaking. Tonya was eleven, Gretchen nine, but only a year back in school. They had everything in their room; a stereo, a computer, even a TV. Jan had insisted. What the hell was the point of a family room if everything they could want was in their bedroom?

Jan was out, probably another late evening appointment to show a house. Her schedule was as hectic as his, but she always reserved time to take the girls to school in the mornings, and be home at 5:30 to fix them supper. He would have to tell her everything about this morning. Little got past her anyway. She was sharp and perceptive—qualities that contributed to her success as a real estate agent. Jan was a multi-million dollar Realtor in both listings and sales. In her mind, her stellar reputation was her most valuable asset. If he were the cause of even the slightest blemish to cloud her name, hot coals would rain upon his head,

Michael toyed with the last few strands of spaghetti in the bowl. They were cold, and he wasn't going to eat them, but he stirred and watched them slide back to the bottom of the bowl. Then stirred and watched some more.

He heard a car pull into the garage.

Jan scurried into the kitchen, her expression tense as though she had a hundred tasks to attend to in the next five minutes. Michael sat amazed how she was always full of energy, even at the end of the day. He was usually exhausted.

She dropped a stack of folders on the kitchen

counter and reached into the refrigerator for a bottle of Sprite. "Got an offer on the Hewes property: $344,900, and another listing on Maplewood," she said between sips of soda.

Michael got up and rinsed the bowl out in the sink. "I have to talk to you."

"Can't it wait? I'm swamped with paperwork."

"No." He rubbed his upper lip as though he had developed an itch.

"Okay, what is it?"

"There was a shooting today." He paused. "It was such a freak deal. I still can't believe it happened."

Jan sat in a kitchen chair and screwed the lid on the plastic bottle. She waited—all of ten seconds. "You can't believe what happened?"

"A teenage boy was hit in the upper leg."

Jan's gaze searched his face and immediately got the drift. "And you did it?"

"It was my gun."

"What do you mean it was your gun? It just went off in your holster?"

Michael sighed. He could deal with deadbeat taxpayers from every occupation and background, but he couldn't find a level playing field to discuss matters with his wife.

"No, it didn't just go off, but it was an accident. The boy's father was threatening me with a rolling pin, and I was trying to stay clear of him and protect myself."

"Oh, jeez, well that explains it," she said. "You could have been attacked with something equally deadly like a soup ladle." The exasperation in her eyes turned to utter contempt. What Jan understood about his job, she despised anyway. Now she was connecting the dots. "You're going to get your name in the paper, aren't you? You'll probably be the lead story in tomorrow's Metro section. 'IRS Agent Michael Cranfield Shoots Unarmed Teenager.' He was unarmed, right?"

"Jan, please. I wanted you to know. I don't know what's going to happen."

"Well, it's going to be in the paper, Michael, you can be sure of that. I hope to high heaven they don't mention you by name. Thanks for the great news. It tops off my day."

Jan picked up her stack of folders and headed to her office down the hall. Michael watched her go, relieved at least he'd told her, then realized she'd walk out of the room on him.

"Jan, that's not all." He followed her and stood in the doorway as she fell into her desk chair.

"What else is it, Michael? I have a closing at ten in the morning, and I have to get this offer ready before that."

"Me, Jan, that's what. I shot a kid today, and I feel terrible. Can't you cut me some slack and tell me everything will turn out all right, even if it's a lie?"

For a moment, she looked at him, and her demeanor softened. He could tell her mind was accessing, searching for the appropriate words to expedite their touchy conversation.

"Michael, you know I've been busy. I'm sorry I acted unsympathetically. I don't want you to get into trouble, and I'm sorry to hear about what happened."

He sat on a stool near her desk. "How have we gotten this way where we hardly talk to each other, and when we do, it seems like we're always raising our voices?"

"Schedules and responsibilities take over the free and easy days of college life," she said. "We have two girls to raise, you know, bills to pay. Things change when you have a career, and other people expect certain things from you. That's just the way it is."

"I remember when you used to laugh at all of my jokes . . ."

"Oh, Michael, please. I told you, I'm busy. I don't have time tonight for some stroll down memory lane. I've always said you're a good father. I don't know what else I can say. As far as I'm concerned, you're in a shady part of government service anyway, and that gun has always made me nervous." She leaned over and gave him a perfunctory peck on the cheek as much to tell him she wanted him to leave as it was an expression of concern. "Please go lie down or take a shower and go to bed. Get a good night's sleep. There's nothing you can do until tomorrow." She turned back to her stack of folders.

Michael left the room, stood in the hall and rubbed his face with both hands, removed his tie, rolled it up, and stuck it in his jacket pocket. It occurred to him that Jan hadn't asked once about the condition of the Dixon boy.

CHAPTER SEVEN

$

A T THE POLICE STATION, early the next day after the shooting, Detective Collins was on the phone when Captain Ross approached his desk.

"The Chief wants to see you," Ross said.

"Why didn't you just call?"

"He wants to see me too."

"I can only imagine what this is about," Collins said.

"A nice big headache you've dumped in the Chief's lap." Ross tapped his notebook in his hand. "Right in here. The Dixon boy."

As they took the elevator up to the seventh floor of Dallas Police Headquarters. Collins second-guessed himself about not requiring the IRS field agents to accompany him to the station yesterday.

He wasn't sure he had the authority to make demands of federal officers, much less arrest them. He let their supervisor, Barnes, call the shots when he should have insisted the agents go with him.

The office of Dallas Police Chief Robert Bentley was a huge room bathed in perpetual sunlight, full of ostentatious plaques, awards, and pictures. Bentley was a big man, tall and muscular with graying hair. When Detective Collins and Captain Ross entered, Bentley was on the phone. His polished silver badge glistened on a tailored and crisp blue uniform. His collar appeared as stiff as sheet metal. Even the buttons on his uniform seemed to stand at attention. It wasn't a sin to walk into his office unannounced when you were expected. Bentley motioned for them to sit as he put down the receiver.

"I see you responded to a shooting involving an IRS agent," Bentley said. "Tell me about it."

Collins related Cleet Dixon's story as well as the implications of the evidence found at the scene. "What I don't know is why it came to such a point. I intend to interview the three agents in more detail today."

"I see," said Bentley. "I got a call from the DA's office this morning. They're already in the middle of this. They're sending someone over now to give me the details."

Collins felt his forehead crinkle as he heard the news. He glanced at Captain Ross and shrugged. They both knew when the DA's office got involved in a case before the investigation was complete, it usually meant the case had jumped to a political track.

Chief Bentley went to the window and gazed out at the pedestrians that milled in and out of city hall. A minute later the door opened, and a man in a three-piece suit entered. It was Melvin Stotler, an assistant district attorney. Collins knew him all too well. He didn't care for either his ability as a courtroom prosecutor or his general attitude. The man was smug and self-righteous. He helped more defendants walk than a physical therapist and seemed hell-bent on letting even serious charges move through the courts with no more than a fine and a slap on the wrist.

"Good morning, gentlemen," Stotler said. Chief Bentley returned to his plush swivel chair.

Collins noted in awe how Stotler's jaw and chin looked as if they'd never seen a whisker, smooth and white as a baby's butt. His head sported a thin layer of blond transparent tufts that gave the illusion of hair, but actually, the man was quite bald. Collins despised the man because he took credit for the accomplishments of others, and he never shut up. Stotler must have friends in the corridors of city hall because, from Collins perspective, Stotler didn't get where he was on merit.

"I understand you have something for us on the Dixon matter," the Chief said.

"Yes, well, in a nutshell, you can close the Dixon file. It's going to be handled internally by the IRS."

"What," exclaimed Collins. He'd anticipated the tone this meeting would take, but he hadn't expected a blatant directive from the DA's office. "The Feds are going to investigate themselves?

You've got to be kidding."

"Our office will keep on top of it," Stotler said, "I assure you."

"You don't assure me of anything, Mr. Stotler. Haven't you heard, we're supposed to have them in custody before you let them go."

"Okay, detective," the Chief said. "Let the assistant DA finish."

"The Dallas office is devastated by this mishap. The IRS is not in the business of jeopardizing the safety of the public. It was an unfortunate incident."

"The publicity isn't real good either." Collins glanced at Ross, who returned a wry smile.

"All medical bills will be taken care of for the Dixon family," Stotler said. "The Service knows they have liability here, and they'll take care of it. This is not a criminal matter."

"Mr. Stotler, let's get real," Collins said. "This is the IRS we're talking about, not some grocer who spilled a bushel of oranges on a little old lady. That's a liability. This is, well? I don't know. Our investigation isn't complete."

Collins turned and faced Bentley. "Chief, I don't know if the agent fired his weapon intentionally or accidentally, and I want to get to the bottom of it. Until our independent investigation is complete, no one can say whether or not this is a criminal matter. Isn't that our job?"

"Chief Bentley, I can answer that if I may," Stotler interrupted. "I see the Service's attitude toward the handling of this matter as something to be expected. The fact that this police department no longer assists them in serving papers and completing property seizures supports their stance on this matter. If Dallas police had assisted with the Dixon property seizure we'd know what happened because we'd have had department personnel on scene. As it is, they have to send Special Agents to assist Revenue Officers. And from the looks of things, that's the way it's going to work for the foreseeable future.

"Anyway, they have an Internal Affairs Division to investigate incidents like this. Bottom line, if the police department isn't going to help them out and they have to put their Special Agents on escort detail, then I can see why they intend to handle this investigation internally."

"What the hell does that have to do with anything, Chief? Everyone at city hall knows your department doesn't have enough police officers as it is. The fact that you no longer lend beat cops to help the Service collect taxes isn't a good reason to allow them to investigate themselves. We have a responsibility in this, Chief." Collins railed. The detective couldn't have been more demonstrative if he'd been preaching a hell, fire, and brimstone sermon at a Sunday service.

"The feds have internal investigators," Stotler said, a smug attitude dripped from his words.

"Yeah, a bunch of professional fixers who know nothing first hand about this incident. Let me finish our investigation, Chief. The feds can do what they want. But a boy's been shot and I don't think the Federal Agent who shot him was justified or restrained in his actions."

Chief Bentley listened without comment,

maintaining his stoic bearing.

"You're wasting your time, detective. The DA is dropping the matter." With that, Stotler picked up his briefcase and walked from the room.

CHAPTER EIGHT

$

BECKY ATTENDED SOUTHERN METHODIST UNIVERSITY at the campus in the heart of Dallas. Her major was interior design. She had three classes today, back to back. She wanted to talk to Matt. If she didn't run into him sooner, she would see him at their business law class at eleven.

In the business law lecture hall, Matt was a no-show. His absence made her more determined to track him down and force a conversation. His car was in the drive at his off-campus condo, and she laid into the doorbell until he answered. Past noon, still in a T-shirt and gym shorts, hair uncombed, eyes glued shut.

"Why didn't you make it to class?"

"Guess I had a few too many last night."

"In the middle of the week? That's not like you and you have practice this afternoon. What's the matter?"

He sat on the edge of a clothes-littered couch and rubbed his sleepy face with both hands. He couldn't raise his head to face her and mumbled at the floor.

"I got a shock yesterday, you know. It just caught me off guard and got me thinking."

"That's good, Matthew, thinking is good. You're talking about the baby, right?"

"Yeah . . . the baby." He looked at her with a dumbstruck expression as though the word held a concept he'd been unable to comprehend until now.

Becky was taken back by what she saw but remained calm. This cock-sure jock with the quick wit and grandiose plans was nothing but a mama's boy without an ounce of backbone when it came to responsibility.

"You know, this baby is ours. I'm in this with you," she said.

"A baby, Becky . . . really? I'm not half-way to my degree. I can't quit now and look for a job to support a kid. I have to get my degree. And—I'm not even sure about that."

"What? I thought you wanted to be an architect?"

"I don't know. I'm taking the basic courses for now, but I'm not sure."

"That's fine. I'll take a break from school and get a part time job."

"What about being an interior designer?"

"It'll take me a little longer; that's all," she said.

"That's nonsense. You're so naive, Becky. Do

you think you can get a job that would pay enough for us to have an apartment and care for an infant at the same time? It ain't happening."

"Yes, I can. You're just thinking of the easy way out. Why can't you accept the idea that life tosses you challenge every once in a while?"

"I'm dying of thirst."

"Sit still. I'll get you a glass of water." Within seconds Becky was back from the kitchen.

Matt drank the whole glass in one gulp, then looked up at his girlfriend. "Why is a baby so important to you now?"

She knelt beside him and placed her hand on his knee. Sunlight through the blinds shown upon her face and her voice carried the conviction of every loving mother from over the centuries, "because it's OUR baby." Her cherubic smile and expression remained as she searched his face for a hint of agreement.

All Matt could do was shake his head and scowl. "You're such a dreamer. I barely turned twenty. I don't want to be tied down with kids."

"So what is it you want?" she said.

"Well, you know what I want." He tried to smile. "I want you in the stands when we play TCU Saturday. Rusty and his girlfriend are going to the lake on Sunday. He's got his dad's boat for the entire day, and they want us to come along. That's what I want, Becky. I want a little time to enjoy things before everything becomes routine and every day seems the same."

"Is that what you think a career and married life is all about? I feel sorry for you." Becky stood.

"This baby was conceived in love. I thought it would be born in love and raised in love, but all you want to do is wad it up and throw it away like garbage. I can't do that. Even if I have to do it by myself, this child will get a chance to play in the mud, and climb trees, and ride a bike. Life is too precious and beautiful not to let that happen."

Becky waited for a moment and watched Matt kneed his temples and stare at the floor, unable to look her in the face. She let herself out of the apartment.

CHAPTER NINE

$

THE NEXT MORNING, Cleet and Becky hardly spoke to each other except to agree to go to the hospital together to see Lance. They found him sitting in bed, eyes closed, the TV on with the sound muted, a half-eaten breakfast on the tray.

"Good morning, trooper," Cleet said.

"Morning, dad." His face had a pinker glow than yesterday when he came out of sedation, but he was obviously still weak.

"You're looking good, boy. You'll be out of here in no time."

"Dad, what did they do to me?"

"The doctors stitched you up. You're going to be as good as new."

"I mean, what did they have to do? Nobody will

tell me anything. These nurses look at me like I'm the sorriest little creature they ever saw."

Cleet couldn't maintain his easy-going expression. His face tightened. "You got shot, boy. A son-of-a-bitch from the government shot you."

"I know, but . . . what did it do to me?"

"They got the bullet out and stitched you up." Cleet coughed into his tightened fist and took a deep breath.

"I can hardly feel a thing, except being sick to my stomach."

"You're awake and talking." Becky smiled at him and brushed her fingers through his hair. "The bullet hit your hip bone. The doctors removed some bone fragments, but your leg is fine. You should make a full recovery." She coated her hopes in positive words as she continued to stroke his head. Lance stared at the ceiling as he listened.

"I'm going to make sure that government son-of-a-bitch goes to jail, son. I promise you that. He had no right to fire his gun; no right at all."

"Daddy, relax," Becky said. "You don't need to get yourself all wound up first thing in the morning."

"Becky, would you come with me—to visit Mother?"

"I have class in an hour."

"You can skip it one time. I need you to come with me this morning."

Cleet took Lance's hand. "I'll be back later, trooper." Becky leaned over the bed rail and kissed Lance on the cheek and followed her father out the door.

Before they arrived at the florist, Becky began to dread what they were about to do. She knew what her father was going to put himself through. Hadn't the last few days been stressful enough? She had agreed too easily to go with him. There was nothing special about today that he should put himself through the sorrow that always accompanied his visits to the cemetery. Today, this wasn't a good idea at all. At the florist, he ordered the same arrangement: hyacinths and lilies. Back in the car, Becky spoke up, "Daddy, today is not a good day to do this. Let's take these flowers to Lance's room."

Cleet was mute. They drove into the cemetery in silence. By now, Becky knew his mind was focused on a solemn duty, commemoration of his only love, a ritual etched in his brain and burned in his soul. A train wreck beyond the black iron fence surrounding the hallowed ground would not have diverted his attention. The cemetery was awash in a sea of pruned and manicured lawns and trees. Along the narrow footpaths were white marble benches. Here and there, freshly cut flowers in bronze vases above recessed markers gave a smattering of pastel colors against the blanket of green.

Across a wooden bridge that spanned a trickle of a stream was her mother's grave. Every time her father's footstep hit that bridge, a wave of sorrow seemed to descend upon him. Her mother had left him too soon. A drunk driver had left him alone with two children to raise. At the cemetery he became a shell of a man; at the cemetery, his dynamic character melted away like hot wax.

Becky remembered in the years before Lance

was born, the three of them would ride through city parks and pose for pictures in their Sunday best. At the swimming pool, he would carry her through the water along the red warning buoys that marked the deep end. Submerged to his chest, water splashed under her chin, but Becky felt no fear. She was in daddy's arms. When they approached the shallow end of the pool, her mother's smile awaited them, and her parents kissed and sunbathed as she played in the shallow water at their feet.

Today, Cleet set the vibrant spray of purple and white flowers in the vase. He sat in the grass and adjusted every petal and stem, oblivious to the grass stains grinding into his khaki pants. He ran his fingers along the edge of the marker set in the ground below the vase.

His life, his business, his children—-everything he did these days sapped his energy, soured his outlook, and disappointed his expectations. None of this would have happened if his dear Nancy hadn't died.

A drunk driver ran a red light and hit Nancy's car square in the driver's side door. Nancy was knocked unconscious and suffered a broken back and ribs. She was in a coma throughout the hospital stay—lingering—a breathing vegetable. Every passing day increased the agony for Cleet. He prayed constantly and willed in his mind that her condition would improve. Though he kissed her and talked to her, she never opened her eyes. Her hands were cool to the touch. The doctors said there was brain activity, but Nancy never regained consciousness. After twenty-eight days, her body gave out, and she died. Cleet was devastated.

Becky looked like her mother. For her father, the loss of his only love was excruciating. The constant reminder of his loss became increasingly difficult to bear.

That was five years ago. Intellectually, he had the best interests of Becky and Lance at heart. But, with Nancy gone, it wasn't the same. He no longer felt the same way about his children. As hard as he tried, he didn't feel the same way about anyone. Becky knew he was at the end of his ability to cope. And now, his son was in the hospital with an uncertain prognosis. Lance was injured by the careless behavior of another criminal individual. If Lance didn't make it, her father would be crushed.

Sadness welled up inside Becky. Watching her father grieve was a display she could barely endure, and today, he was putting himself through it again. Her father's sorrow had not diminished one bit since the day the two of them and Lance sat on folding chairs in a green tent erected on this very spot.

"I'm trying so hard, baby," he said. "Sometimes it all becomes too much. It seems like I'm forced to be a juggler and keep a hundred balls in the air. When you were here, I could juggle them all."

Becky had to walk away. She walked through the trees and went through a wad of tissues as she dabbed her eyes. When she returned to the grave, he was still seated in the grass running his fingers along the edge of the marker. Becky helped her father back to his Cadillac, and she drove them back to the hospital.

****

"Are you going to stay here for the rest of the day?" Becky asked her father as they pulled into the hospital parking lot.

Cleet nodded.

"I need to take the car to school for an hour, but I'll go with you up to the room."

"Go ahead," he said, as he sniffed and wiped the corner of his eye. "I'm going to find someone to give me an update on Lance."

When Becky entered the room, she saw the back of a man standing at Lance's bedside.

"I'm relieved to see you're doing well. I'm so sorry for what happened," the man said.

Lance's face twisted in an expression of utter loathing. "This is the man who shot me," he said when he saw his sister.

When the man turned toward the door, Becky recognized him instantly. Here was the man who showed up at her home ready to take almost everything of value they owned. Five feet from where she stood was the man who shot her brother. Her eyes widened as a scramble of thoughts raced through her brain.

"You shouldn't be here," she said breathlessly. "My father's in the building."

"I'll go. I had to know he was all right."

Becky shook her head. "All right? You've got to be the stupidest person on the face of the earth to call his condition all right."

Michael turned to leave as the door swung open.

Cleet walked in, head down, wiping his nose with a tissues. His bearing instantly changed from sorrow to rage as he recognized who was in the room.

"What the hell are you doing here? Get your worthless, filthy, money grubbing ass. . ." Cleet lunged at Michael and knocked him against the back wall. Cleet's arm caught an armful of the curtain divider with his forward momentum, and it tore loose as he fell forward.

Michael jumped to the side. "Get a grip, Dixon. I just came to wish your son the best." Michael managed to grab the portable tray table and keep it in front of him as he backed toward the door. "It was an accident."

"Get out and stay out. We don't need your self-serving lies."

Cleet panted as he stared at the closing door. A moment later, he grabbed the door handle and dashed down the corridor. He took the stairwell, bounded down two steps at a time, stepped into the lobby, and saw Michael walk out the front of the building. Cleet followed. He held back enough to remain unseen. In the parking lot, Cleet saw what he wanted to know. Michael slipped behind the seat of a silver Acura. Cleet moved behind a row of bushes as the Acura pulled from the parking space. Cleet could see the back of the car, tag number—Texas V20 DJC.

He returned to Lance's room and stayed with him while Becky went to the university. But now that he had Cranfield's car tag number, he was too keyed up to spend the rest of the day twiddling away the hours in the hospital. He wanted to know where Cranfield lived. Where did he spend his time? What places did he frequent? Where might he be alone or accessible and vulnerable?

Cleet wrote down the address of every Cranfield listed in the Dallas phone directories. He knew many people used cell phones exclusively, but many still had land lines at home. His list came to nineteen Cranfield listings. There were five phone numbers that used an initial for a first name, which were probably single women, and three without addresses. A federal employee would surely have a home phone number though it may be unlisted. He would worry about that later. Almost as an afterthought, Cleet made a note of a 2 X 3-inch display ad in the white pages.

IMAGINATION HOMES
Jan Cranfield, REALTOR
"Live Your Dreams"

The ad included an address for the agency, as well as home and work numbers. Cleet looked up the business address on his map. Right in the heart of North Dallas. He placed the address near the top of his list.

As soon as Becky returned from her class, Cleet took his car keys and left with nothing more than a perfunctory "I'll be back later," to Becky and Lance. He drove to a 'Cranfield address' closest to the hospital. It was an older home that hadn't seen a paintbrush in years. The single car garage was closed. The grass was dotted with patches of brown. Even the weeds needed water. Cleet parked across the street and walked to the curbside mailbox as a teenage boy, about fifteen, came around the house.

"Hey, what' ya doing?"

Cleet instantly knew the queasy feeling of getting caught with his hand in the cookie jar. "I wasn't going to take anything," he said.

"Yeah, so what' ya doing? The boy kept his distance, but his gaze fixed in an unflinching stare. "That's a crime opening someone's mailbox, ya know."

"I know. That was dumb. I should have knocked on the door. I wanted to see if this was the Cranfield residence."

"Yeah, so what?"

"I'm from out of town, and I wasn't sure of the address. I'm a friend of your dad's. Is he home?"

The kid waited a moment, and then a knowing smirk broke across his face. "You're full of shit, mister. My dad don't live here, never has. You better leave before I call the cops."

Cleet hustled back to his car and backed down the street. At the first intersection, he rolled around the corner, yanked the car into drive, and lost no time getting out of the neighborhood.

A few miles west, he found another address on his list. Two cars sat in the drive; neither a silver Acura. He realized he needed to stop for gas soon. Locating Cranfield's home would take time and energy. He didn't care how long it took. As dusk fell, Cleet still cruised the streets of North Dallas, peering at strange houses, studying cars that sat in darkened driveways. By midnight he was exhausted. He pulled behind a one-story office building with a FOR SALE sign taped to the front door, stretched out in the front seat of the Cadillac, and fell asleep.

CHAPTER TEN

$

ICHAEL HARDLY SLEPT, listening to Jan's sporadic snores in the next bed. Mental pictures of Dixon's living room, Dixon's tirade, and the rolling pin swinging high in the air played over and over in his mind during fitful sleep. He heard the blast from his handgun and the sickening thuds of the boy falling down the steps.

Yesterday, Barnes had read him the riot act but hadn't suspended him, at least not yet. He was about to leave the house when Frank called and asked him to meet him at the I-HOP off the south freeway in Oak Cliff. Michael arrived first and waited in a back booth amid the snap of newspapers and the bustle of humanity that churned the smell of bacon grease and maple syrup.

Why did Frank play mind games with every taxpayer he dealt with? What was the point? Everyone they met was going to be stressed out. Why make it worse? It was their job to collect money, but why the need to ruin a person's day or give them an ulcer by jerking their strings?

Michael was fully aware that many of the people they dealt with were criminals, pure and simple, con men and scammers who only responded to force. But there were others who were just trying to make ends meet. They would pay their federal taxes if given a way out. To make them physically sick with threats of huge fines and jail time only made matters worse.

Frank walked in with a 7-11 travel mug and helped himself from the coffee pitcher on the table. "I've already eaten." He grabbed a wad of sugar packets, lined them up, tore them open, and shook them into his mug. "Ready?

"I'm almost finished." He could tell Frank was impatient to tell him something, but Frank was reluctant to talk shop in a public place. Michael stuffed a final fork of pancakes into his mouth and washed it down with a gulp of coffee.

Frank drove a faded orange-tan Buick that was probably the biggest thing on four wheels that GM ever built. It was old, ugly, and a rolling litter bag. Apparently, Frank spent half of his life in the car. The back seat was full of boxes, a change of clothes hung on the hook behind his seat. He used the passenger seat as a medicine cabinet and the floor as a trash receptacle. Every time Michael rode with him, it took several minutes to carve out enough room for him to get in the car.

"Got a phone call this morning," Frank said as they pulled from the restaurant parking lot and headed south on I-35.

"About what?"

"About you. Barnes wanted a little one-on-one without your ears present. I told him the same story as yesterday. Hey, I understand what happened, Cranfield. I know you wish it hadn't happened, but it was justified. I was there. I saw it."

"It was an accident."

"Whatever you say."

"What's going to happen?"

"In the long run, probably nothing. Barnes is playing it by the book."

"How long am I going to be under the microscope?"

"A few weeks, maybe a month," Frank said. "This is where our zombie friends from IRS Internal Affairs earn their keep. Even if it isn't classified an accident, they'll list it as justified. No one got killed. Take my word for it. That's what the final report will say." He pulled a half-smoked White Owl from the ashtray and lit it. "Back when I shot that biker, the department asked questions, filled out forms, and processed the whole incident like it was another day at the office. Once the smoke cleared, they brought me back."

The smoke wasn't clearing now, the car filled with plumes. Michael cracked his window. Frank leaned back behind the wheel like he was reliving a good movie.

"I'll tell you something else," Frank said. "That

Dixon prick hasn't seen the last of us. It won't be long before other agents will take a truck to that house and get the items on that forfeiture list. Barnes is just waiting, probably until the kid's out of the hospital—then it's business as usual."

"My wife has a love/hate attitude about what I do, but I can't lose this job," Michael said. "She hates that I carry a gun, but she loves the government benefits. She'll kill me if I get fired."

"Good grief, Cranfield, would you take it easy?"

"Have you ever pulled your weapon any other time?" Michael asked.

"Yeah, several times," Frank said. "But in the line of duty, I only fired it against that biker."

"I wondered—the way you jaw with some of these people."

Frank glanced at Michael, and his expression changed.

"Cranfield, ole boy, once you've been at this business as long as I have, you'll have a different attitude about these deadbeats."

"But why do you go out of your way to get people all worked up and out of sorts?"

Frank let out a hoot and sat up in his seat. "I've never said everyone should work like I do. I just know what works for me."

"To get people stressed out when they probably have enough to deal with already?" Michael shook his head in disbelief.

"Now listen up, and listen good. Your mopey, soft-hearted whining isn't going to serve you at all. By the time we get our cases, the people know the drill. These aren't some little old ladies who forgot to put their social security number on their tax return."

"These deadbeats are trying to get away without paying their taxes. Everyone knows if they earn income or make a business profit, they owe taxes on that money. It flat-out burns my ass how some of these people are so blatant in trying to get away with it."

"I don't cut them any slack because they don't deserve any. If delinquent taxpayers think you'll buy a sob story or some other line of crap, that's all you'll get. By the time we see them, they're full of excuses. They've rationalized all of their dodges and delays until they have themselves deluded. It's my job to deliver a dose of reality. No more excuses. No more delays. Pay up or close up."

"Yeah, I get the picture."

"Hey, it's not my picture, pal. It's Uncle Sam's picture. Somebody has to collect the money. That's why you're here and don't ever forget it. You getting soft after yesterday?"

"No, I know what our job is," Michael said.

"Take for example this guy we're going to see. I've talked to him on the phone several times, and I know he's received a basket full of letters from Austin. He thinks ignoring our notices is as inconsequential as failing to RSVP a dinner party. Well, he's about to find out he's made a big mistake. I intend to raise his blood pressure about fifty points."

"Think about it this way, Cranfield, Uncle Sam is one big credit card company. Okay, now once you charge against that card, the company is looking for its money back plus interest." Frank stared through the windshield and chomped on the cigar stub that had gone out long ago. "If you don't pay your credit card bill, the financial company loses money. They cancel the card and charge off the loss. End of story.

"But with the federal government, citizens continue to receive benefits even when they don't pay their share. Most benefits people don't think about every day—a military to protect our borders, the FAA to keep planes from flying into one another, a department that inspects the food we eat, and another that inspects the pills we take. The list goes on and on.

"If you don't pay your taxes, you still receive the benefits. The federal government can't write off the bills of those who cheat or refuse to pay. Uncle Sam has to get the money because money is being spent. So, in addition to the audit department, there's us. An enforcement division is critical. We have to feed the beast because no one would pay more than a token amount to Washington if we weren't around."

"I know all of that," Michael said, glad that Frank had run out of steam. Michael understood their mission. He hadn't cared about Frank's antagonistic antics with taxpayers—until now. The hollow sense of guilt was more than he could continue to endure ever since his stray bullet hit an innocent kid. He would make restitution to the Dixon family. He would get the Dixon forfeiture list dropped from the IRS database.

If he was caught, not only would he be fired, he would be prosecuted. But he had to do it. He had to try. It was the only way he could absolve his guilt. It was the only way he could make meaningful restitution.

"Ah, here it is," Frank said, "11650 Fox Run Road as he pulled into the parking lot.

Michael read the sign painted on the building: SAUNDERS PRINTING COMPANY.

CHAPTER ELEVEN

$

CLEET AWOKE IN HIS CAR before daybreak and took a minute to orient himself. His mouth was dry, and he had to piss. He used a nearby wooden fence as a urinal and stopped at a 7-11 for coffee and donuts. For the next twenty minutes, he looked up the Cranfield addresses on an old city map and tried to arrange them in an order where he didn't have to waste time driving around. Unless the address was in North Dallas, he omitted it for the time being.

He didn't give his wrinkled, slept-in clothes a second thought, his children, or the hospital. His energy was focused on finding a silver Acura. Cleet circled the first address on his list, a house on Ridgedale Drive.

****

Michael heard Jan leave more than an hour ago as he rolled over in bed. Now he awoke to an empty house. Weekends were always her busiest days showing homes and holding open houses. Tonya and Gretchen were at a slumber party, so most of Saturday would be history before they returned.

He stared at the ceiling and thought how his girls were so aloof with him, polite but distant, even at such young ages. Daddy was there, a familiar fixture around the house, but with no real function. Their mother was a breadwinner too and the girls knew it. She accommodated their fashion whims, club dues, field-trip money, and whatever desires crossed their prepubescent minds. Michael knew he needed to get more involved in his daughter's lives.

But at this moment, he had a more pressing concern. His job was in jeopardy. The clandestine inner workings of the Service would decide his fate. He had reason to be more fearful of that arrangement than having the civilian justice system adjudicate his punishment. Maybe the Service would transfer him to another department. If so, he'd keep his time in grade. But what if the boy died or the heat from upstairs got too hot for Barnes. All allegiances to him would dissipate like smoke in a whirlwind, and Barnes would hand him a pink slip with no more ceremony than a teacher issuing a hall pass..

He had promised Jan he would stain the wood railings around the back porch. The project would give him something to do. He pulled his Acura from the garage so he could get to his tools in the cabinets along the wall.

As he was preparing the tools he needed, a faded green sedan pulled along the curb and Detective Collins stepped out. Collins surveyed the house as he walked slowly into the garage. "Morning, Mr. Cranfield. I want to ask you a few general questions about the incident if you don't mind?"

Michael nodded. He knew the Service had taken over the thrust of the investigation and he'd rather do anything than talk to the cops. But stonewalling the local police might not be a good choice in the long run. "What do you want to know?" Michael said as he turned back to the workbench.

"I've never heard your side of the story. It's my job and my nature to ask questions. I'd like you to tell me what happened."

"Plain and simple, Detective. Mr. Dixon couldn't handle the fact that the jig was up on his tax delinquency and continual delays. He threw a glass ashtray at me and knocked me across the kitchen floor."

"Couldn't you have backed away and called in additional manpower?"

"That's not our standard procedure. We're federal officers serving an authorized administrative property seizure. The man didn't want to face reality, so he started what I can only describe as an adult tantrum."

Collins wrote notes on a spiral pad. "All right, Mr. Dixon was upset at your presence. You've seen that before, right?"

"Most certainly," Michael said.

"Were you at any time afraid your life was in danger?"

Michael walked to the garage entrance and took in a deep breath of cool morning air. "I know where you're going with this, and I can't let you frame those events as though I used a flimsy excuse to use deadly force against the guy. I intended to hold back until he blew off some steam. I was in a confined space. He was directing all of his hostility at me. He threw a butcher knife at me. Did you know that?"

Collins kept writing.

"I deeply regret it. I wouldn't wish that on any family. I have children of my own."

"Okay," Collins said, "You didn't feel immediately threatened, at least not for your life. After all, your partner was standing right there. So, why did you pull your weapon?"

Michael scowled. Maybe talking to this gumshoe was a bad idea. If he thought he'd be playing to a sympathetic ear, he was badly mistaken. "Haven't you ever drawn your handgun and not used it?" Michael asked.

"No, not that I can recall," Collins said. "But that's what you did. That's what you're telling me, right? You drew your .38, but you didn't intend to use it?"

Michael swallowed. "Yeah, yeah, that's what I'm telling you."

"But you did use it, didn't you?" Collins pressed him now. "It didn't go off by accident. You meant to fire. Dixon was getting too close, and you got scared, right?"

Collins went silent and focused his unflinching gaze like a laser. Michael thought the whole neighborhood went quiet. He had to respond. The silence became an unbearable weight while his mind centered on that one moment in time when his actions harmed an innocent kid. Collins waited.

The dam finally broke. "YES, I fired it."

"At Mr. Dixon?"

"No, I wouldn't do that. Not unless he went for the gun."

"So who were you firing at?"

Again silence. This time Collins didn't wait him out. "Who were you firing at, Cranfield? Who was it?"

"No one. It just went off."

"Listen to yourself, Cranfield. You and I both know your gun didn't just go off. Who were you firing at?"

"It was a warning shot." Michael's voice trailed off. He'd gotten nervous and shot into the air to slow Dixon down and bring him to his senses.

Collins stopped. He had his answer. He didn't need to ask more questions. A federal agent had fired his gun toward the ceiling in a two-story house. That was bad enough. The bullet could have injured or killed someone on the second floor. But Cranfield's shot hadn't even hit the ceiling. His half-cocked shot hit a boy sitting on the staircase.

Collins slipped his notepad into his jacket pocket. He watched Michael walk back to the workbench and drop his face into his hands. The man looked truly exhausted and guilt-ridden. But absolution was not part of Collin's job description. Cranfield would have to work through his emotions on his own terms and in his own time.

"My department is not officially investigating

this matter. I figure you know that," Collins said. "I came here this morning to get a clearer picture of what happened to satisfy my own curiosity. You won't see me again. It's probably just as well your agency is dealing with this matter. Carelessness may not be a crime, Mr. Cranfield, but you better pray that boy makes it. If he doesn't, I figure your troubles are just beginning.

CHAPTER TWELVE

$

WATCHING COLLINS DRIVE AWAY gave Michael a measure of relief. What he admitted, he had always known. He had gotten nervous and fired his revolver. He hadn't even aimed. He just pulled the trigger. He didn't want to think about that morning again, but he couldn't escape the reality of how careless he had been.

Michael set about staining the back patio railing, then made himself a sandwich, and took a nap. Anything to free his mind. When he awoke it was almost one. He got in his car and drove west on LBJ Freeway. Sugars was a long drive closer to downtown, but the time in the car gave him time to daydream and listen to classical music on the radio. He hoped Elaine worked on Saturdays, though he knew it was unlikely she'd be there at this early hour.

"But Elaine was at the club, saw him as soon as he walked in, and strolled over with a sexy curl to her lips that made him relax. She wore a frilly, blue, mid-thigh, cocktail dress with a tiny white apron. "Nice to see you, Michael. Is Frank with you?"

"No, I came by myself. I hoped you were working today." His depressing thoughts disappeared. "I'll take a margarita."

"Want to go in the back? I don't go on for thirty minutes."

He nodded.

"Go on back. I'll get your drink."

Michael disappeared into another room behind the thick curtain. Elaine walked over and whispered to Byron, who held court from his permanent vantage point behind the DJ platform. Byron was part owner and official bouncer. At 6'6' and 270 pounds, Byron could lift the average patron by the collar, escort him to the parking lot, and invite him back with such affability that once the man sobered up, he'd look forward to returning. On the other hand, Byron could crack a walnut with two fingers. Elaine told him she had a special client in the back and to leave her out of the rotation until they came out front.

Except for Michael and Elaine, the back room was empty. A half dozen other round tables bolted to the floor filled the room, each with a single spotlight that shown down on each one. Life size silver cutouts of naked women adorned the walls.

"Been keeping busy?" Elaine sat the margarita

on the table and scooted her chair beside him.

Michael nodded.

"Glad you didn't stay away too long," she said.

Michael took a long swig of his tangy cocktail. "I like seeing you."

"Same for me, Michael." She edged closer. "You know, some guys come here who like to watch me dance, and they buy me drinks, but you're the only guy I like to talk to."

There was something about the timing of her words that made them the very thing he needed to hear. Intellectually, he knew she could be spouting an old, sad verse that had been rehearsed and recited to every lonely stiff who walked through the front door. But, right now, Michael didn't care. Elaine sensed his vulnerability and leaned in and kissed his cheek.

For a moment, they gazed at each other. Elaine reached and stroked his cheek with the back of her hand. Michael's cares were washed away. Her fingers lingered on his chin, and she smiled. "I really like you, Michael."

His chest filled with giddy delight. He gulped down the rest of his drink. "I really like you, too."

"Tell me about yourself," she said with a playful pout.

Her request sounded harmless, a natural extension of a casual conversation. He had told her he was married, but Michael didn't want her to know he had two daughters. He wanted the excitement of their liaison blissfully shrouded in ignorance.

But today, of all days, he wanted to speak about

his work. He needed to shed some of the guilt that strangled his heart. Who better to burden than a strange woman who only knew his first name? Here was a woman who got paid whether she stripped or listened to every sob story under the sun. "What do you want to know?" he asked.

"You must be a cop," Her eyes widened and she nodded in anticipation he would confirm her suspicion. "The handgun." She refreshed his memory as she reached inside his thigh and moved her hand up his leg.

"Oh yeah, my gun. No, I'm not a cop."

"Just relax," she whispered. "You're a U.S. Marshall then?"

"I'm an agent for the IRS," Michael said as he stood quickly.

"Ah, the IRS," she said. "You want me to make you feel good?"

"I just want to talk."

"You're sweet, Michael. That's fine if that's what you want."

"I need another drink . . . and one for you too."

"I'll be right back."

Michael rolled the empty tumbler in his hands and thought about the painful truth Detective Collins got him to admit. Elaine returned with two fresh drinks.

"I shot an innocent boy three days ago,"

"Good grief! You killed him?"

"No, he's alive, but in the hospital in a bad way. I was careless. I should never have let it happen." Michael raised his head and searched for a flicker of understanding in Elaine's eyes, and he found it.

"That's so terrible. It must have been an accident."

"That's what I tried to tell myself, but it was plain carelessness."

"I'm so sorry."

"I don't know what to do. I can't sleep. I'm afraid the kid may never walk again, or worse. I've got to do something to even things up—make it right if I can."

Elaine took a sip of her watered-down champagne. "This has to do with your job?"

"Yeah. The kid's father owes a lot in back taxes.."

"Okay, well jeez, Michael, if you didn't do it on purpose, maybe you should get involved in something else to get your mind off it. I mean, there's not much you can do to even things up once you're shot someone—unless, of course, you made the old man's tax problem go away."

Michael's body stiffened, and he almost spilled his drink. She made it sound so simple, no more complicated than hailing a taxi. But to attempt such a thing would be foolhardy. Not only would he lose his career if caught, but he'd quickly land behind bars. "That's not a solution," he said.

"Why not? You can access tax files, can't you? I would think you could make some tax debts disappear and no one would know the difference."

Michael slowly shook his head.

"What I said makes sense, doesn't it?"

"No, it doesn't. I got myself into a jam, but I'm not going to make it worse." Her suggestion grated in his brain because that was exactly what he planned to do. In essence, she gave him permission. It was the only way to make restitution.

"What you need right now is for me to dance for you. We're in here alone. I'll give you a nice show. Take your mind off all your cares and worries, Michael."

"Okay, dance for me. But first, get me another drink. I need another drink."

CHAPTER THIRTEEN

$

CLEET HAD BEEN SITTING IN HIS CAR ever since he found a silver Acura parked in the residential driveway. He watched as a green sedan stopped, a man got out, and he started a conversation with a man in the garage. He thought the man who stopped looked like the detective who was at his house, but he wasn't sure. Many people came and went the morning Lance was shot. He didn't exactly take a close look at everyone who was there.

When the green sedan left, Cleet walked close enough to the back of the Acura to read the license plate—-Texas V20 DJC.

Now he knew where Cranfield lived. He could come back after dark and set the place on fire. He could wait and watch and see if any children went in or out. The thought grew in his heart to maim one of Cranfield's children and let him experience true emotional pain. There was simple, justifiable logic in the idea.

Cleet watched the garage door close with the car still in the driveway. No one else came or left the house. Cleet knew Cranfield was there—maybe alone. Now might be the best time to confront him and knock his teeth out. The urge to move now built within him, grab the guy by the throat at his front door, and beat the shit out of him on his front lawn.

But Cleet remained in the car, staring through the windshield, seething with rage, but unable to move. He didn't want witnesses. He didn't want to be identified by neighbors and brought up on assault charges. A beating was too good for the bastard anyway. Cleet wanted more—to ruin him professionally and financially, and destroy his family. He sat in his car all morning, watching the house, seething and plotting. He wished he had a bomb and knew how to attach it to the underside of a car. He wondered how long it took to attach a bomb to a car and how a bomb was triggered. A needed bathroom break forced him to drive to a nearby Quik Trip. He bought a packaged sandwich, then returned to the house and his parking spot across the street. Not long after he returned, Cranfield opened his front door and walked to the car.

Cleet watched Cranfield get in the Acura and drive away. Cleet stayed behind him, but back far enough to avoid detection. The Acura moved briskly, passing slower traffic with jumps of acceleration. Cranfield's car passed Highway 75, exited at Greenville Avenue, and drove south. Caught by a stoplight, Cleet watched at the intersection as the Acura pulled into a men's club parking lot. Cleet drove slowly by and around the block. As he passed back by the establishment, Cleet pulled through the lot. The Acura was parked. Cranfield had gone inside.

The place was called Sugars. The lot was filling up. Men in need of an afternoon belt of liquor and female titillation sauntered in. The heavy action would begin after dark. The men here now were guys who had to be home by suppertime. A doorman glanced at Cleet as he walked in, but said nothing. Colored strobe lights pulsated over two stages while a hard dance beat pounded ten decibels above loud. Cleet sat in the middle of the room and ordered a Coors.

Once his eyes adjusted to the shadowy interior, he searched the room for Cranfield. Waitresses wearing short, frilly skirts milled around between twenty to thirty men in the place. The young women served drinks and smiled as they stuffed bills into their bras. Cleet summoned a waitress to his table.

Is this the only room in here?" he asked.

"Hi, I'm Amber." The cute blonde placed a coaster on his table and displayed her dazzling teeth in a sly smile. "It is unless you had something special in mind."

Cleet cocked his head. "Like what?"

"Like your own special dance, silly."

He felt a pang of stupidity. For a moment, Cleet had thought of something else. "Where?"

"There's another room over there. Would you like me to dance for you?"

Cleet looked at what appeared to be a solid wall. "Maybe later. Bring me another beer." He handed her a $5 bill and headed to the restroom. On the way back, he worked his way along the dark wall. His hands touched velvet. He pulled back the heavy drape and slipped inside. One table was in use. A dancer was performing for a guy leaned back in his chair, taking it all in. Cleet couldn't be sure it was Cranfield but suspected it was. He would wait around and be sure.

Cleet watched and listened for a minute then went back to his table. So this federal agent got his kicks at a strip joint. What else might he be involved in? It wouldn't be out of the question for him to have a few of the girls find out what patrons had tax problems, then make promises to squelch their tax obligations for a lucrative fee.

Or, it could work the other way, too. In a shady place like this, once someone knew his occupation, they could figure out a way to blackmail Cranfield. His marriage or career could be on the line. Cranfield could be coerced to help someone with their tax problems to keep from being exposed. Cleet's heart warmed to the thought of Cranfield getting job-related criminal charges brought against him. Cranfield's vulnerable underbelly might dwell in the hidden recesses of a strip club like this.

Cleet saw the man and woman from the back room come to the front and he summoned Amber back to his table. "Have you seen that guy before?"

Amber looked the way Cleet was pointing and

gave the guy a once over. "We have a lot of customers here. I see lots of faces."

"Who's he with?"

"That's Elaine."

"Look again. Does he come in here often?" He held a twenty in the air between his fingers.

Amber looked at the man again, and then at the twenty. "Yeah, sure," she said. "He's a regular." She took the bill and stuck it in her bra, rolling her eyes as she walked away.

Cranfield certainly acted like he was a regular and knew his way around. Cleet wanted to dig up any shady associations, unethical dealings, or inappropriate behavior. He needed someone on the inside to watch Cranfield when he was here, see what he was up to, take note of who he met. Cleet dismissed the idea of approaching any of the current waitresses. If they had dealings with Cranfield, they'd ruin the plan. He needed someone new to get a job at the club, someone who would watch Cranfield like a hawk and befriend him.

CHAPTER FOURTEEN

$

FRANK MASTERS WAS IN A BAD MOOD when he awoke Saturday. He had the weekend off, but yesterday his cell phone vibrated on and off all day long. Frank knew who was calling. It pissed him off. No calls during the workweek, that was the deal. Now he had some free time, but he still hadn't returned the call. Raney could wait and worry. Frank didn't jump for anyone.

Bill Raney was a two-bit bookkeeper and tax preparer who completed returns with the speed of an Olympic sprinter and the precision of a drunk walking on ice. If there were gray areas in a tax return, he made them in favor of the IRS. Raney didn't put his ass on the line for anyone unless there was an extra fee involved. He wasn't paid to save people money on their taxes. That malarkey was a myth. He was paid to prepare returns, crunch numbers, push paper. If someone wanted to know the latest tax loophole, let them hire a tax attorney or study the code themselves. He didn't make any money tracking down tax breaks for clients.

But talk about toeing the line was a smoke screen. Raney knew every imaginable way to paste up a tax return, and he was more than willing to do it if the client paid extra. Raney would cheat his mother out of a quarter if he thought he could get away with it. He didn't care if his 'extra fee' came from reduced receipts into the coffers of the U.S. Treasury as long as he got paid. He was always on the lookout for ways to make another dime. It was through this mutual topic of interest Frank and Raney became acquainted.

Three years ago, while investigating a tax return involving significant dollars and dubious deductions, Frank paid a visit to the accountant who had prepared the return. Raney's response to his standard list of questions was different from any Frank had ever heard before. Instead of launching into a diatribe of excuses and double-talk, Raney was open and forthcoming. He admitted that his client's return was questionable and that he had been the preparer. Without so much as a quiver in his voice, Raney bragged about the high fees he was able to charge for such efforts and said he'd be more than willing to split them with an agent who could provide a measure of cover.

Frank had been about to cuff him, but the monetary possibilities aroused his curiosity. There was a pressing reason why Frank might take a risk that could easily put him behind bars. He needed money. His divorce the previous year, after twenty years of marriage, had left him damn near penniless. The bitch got the house, the furniture, and the Ford Explorer. He got the IOU's, the outstanding balances on three credit cards, apartment rent, alimony, and an oil-burning pile of rolling junk.

There was another factor too, and the pasty-faced bookkeeper's spiel hit a nerve. Frank was fed up with the insignificant, automatic civil service pay raises. He'd brought in literally millions of dollars into the U.S. Federal Treasury over his twenty-eight-year career, and he deserved a raise that would buy more than another case of beer a month. So that day, three years ago, Frank listened to the details of Raney's tax schemes and put his badge back in his pocket.

With Frank's muscle and inside knowledge, Raney could get his clients further and further immersed in questionable tax accounting practices until they were utterly beholden to him. As the months and years passed, Raney did just that.

"So what'cha got that you been calling all day?" Frank demanded when Raney answered.

"Ah, nice to hear your voice, my friend. Got a guy who runs a moving company off of Stemmons Freeway. He's got close to thirty employees. He had a company health savings account set up for the past six years, but now he doesn't want to fund it anymore."

Frank understood the implication. If the guy dropped his company health plan, it would cut into

Raney's available skim money because the deductions would change.

"You got the goods on him?" Frank asked.

"Oh yeah, my friend. He's been doing more jobs for cash than a corner lemonade stand, and not reporting a cent."

"Okay, what's the name and address? I'll give him the standard routine."

"Great. 2200 Mockingbird. The last name's Cecil."

"I'll drop by there Monday morning."

****

Becky spent all day Friday at the hospital waiting for her father to return. When visiting hours were over, and Lance was asleep, she called a cab for a ride home. Saturday morning, she drove in her car back to the hospital. Her father hadn't been home all night. He hadn't returned her calls despite repeated messages left on his cell phone. Couldn't he have at least given her a ring saying he wasn't returning to the hospital? When he left, he said he was coming back.

She was increasingly concerned about her father's mental state. More than anything, she wanted to keep the family together. It was an elusive and ever diminishing possibility. Ever since her mother died, events threatened to stretch the bonds that held the three of them together beyond the breaking point.

Lance was wriggling around in bed, trying to adjust his position when Becky came in the room.

"This pillow is as hard as a punching bag," Lance said. "Can you find me something softer?"

"I'll try."

"Help me roll over a bit. No, not that. It'll hurt. Raise me. I've got to arch my shoulders."

Becky pushed the buttons on the bed controller.

"Hand me the water bottle, please."

"Did you sleep well?"

"Kinda—not really. My stomach hurts. They're going to take more x-rays today."

Lance was talking, complaining. That alone would seem to indicate he was making progress. But in the morning light that filled the room, Becky saw her brother's sallow, sweaty face.

"I want to stand as soon as possible. I've got to get on my feet. Will I ever be able to run again?" Lance's voice took on a pleading tone, desperate for affirmation as he looked at his sister.

"Don't get in such a hurry it sets you back," Becky said. "Do what the doctor orders."

A nurse entered the room, a tree stump of a woman with fat pink cheeks and small teeth. A blue-gowned aide followed her in. "It's time to change your dressing." She dropped the side rail with a clank. "Feeling better?"

Lance shook his head. He grimaced as she pulled down his sheets and rolled him onto his side.

She removed the gauze patch. The sewn bullet wound was red and puffy. She cleaned the wound and replaced the dressing. "We better check that diaper of yours, whaddayasay?" She yanked the Velcro strips, and as soon as she pulled back the flap, her face sank. She caught the female aide by the arm and gave her an order in no uncertain terms.

"Hurry and get Dr, Sammons, and Nurse Anders. His stool is full of blood."

Within seconds, Becky was forced into a corner with the rush of attendants filing into the room. She caught a glimpse of Lance's wide eyes as he was wheeled out. All of the frantic activity gripped her with panic The thought crossed her mind Lance was going to die.

Then she was alone. She could hear her rapid breathing, Horrible thoughts cascaded through her brain. She needed Matt; she needed her father. But neither of them were anywhere to be found.

She called her father's cell phone again, but no answer. She had wanted to stay home today, complete college assignments, and make plans for a baby that no one wanted but her. That would have to wait for another day. For now, she sat on the chair, leaned her head against the bed, and prayed with all her heart for the recovery of her injured brother.

She fell asleep in the chair and didn't awake until she heard the massive door push open and the lights click on.

"What's going on? Where's Lance?"

Becky dabbed her eyes with a tissue. "He's back in surgery."

She heard a huge rush of air fill her father's lungs and saw fear etch his face. "What happened?"

"No one has come back to tell me anything. They took him—must have been around 9:00. What time is it now?"

"Geez, Rebecca, did't you find out anything?"

"Oh, Daddy." She grabbed and held him.

Cleet helped her back into the chair, then headed for the nurses' station. He returned a few minutes later, more concern written on his face. They waited in silence as Cleet paced the floor from the window to the door. Finally, an older man in green scrubs came into the room.

"Mr. Dixon, your son is sedated now and will sleep most of the day."

"What happened?" Cleet asked.

"A tear in his intestine ruptured, and we found additional bone splinters. We conducted another colonoscopy and a full set of abdominal x-rays. Hopefully, we got all of the bone fragments. Only time will truly tell."

"You don't know!"

"I know he's fine now," the doctor said.

"For the love of . . ."

"Daddy, they're doing their best."

Cleet ignored her. "Put him back on that gawd damned picture machine until you're sure."

"As I said, he's going to be sleeping all day. Why don't you go get some rest yourself and come back this evening." The doctor turned and left the room.

"Let's go home," Becky said. "Let's get out of here for a while. Lance is sleeping." She pulled on her father's elbow elbow.

Cleet looked at her with an expression of total confusion. The sight of Becky seemed to engage his brain on a topic heavy on his mind, but until now, derailed by Lance's emergency.

"I need to talk to you," he said. Cleet grabbed the

foot rail as he gathered his thoughts.

Cleet looked at his daughter. Even without makeup, her natural beauty was evident — the tanned glow of her skin she had inherited from her mother. Her short, dark hair framed a delicate nose and chin. Her expressive brown eyes confessed her every emotion.

"I found out where the creep who shot Lance spends his time," Cleet said. "From what I gathered, he spends much of his free time at a gentleman's club on Greenville Avenue. That's the kind of place where he could be selling his inside knowledge or getting people off the hook with the IRS, and yet, honest folk still have to pay all their taxes."

"A gentleman's club?" Becky asked.

"Yeah, it's a smoky bar for businessmen in suits. A place to drink and socialize. I need someone to get a job there, wait tables most likely, and make friends with this guy when he comes around."

"Then what?"

"Find out what he's up to. You know he's a coward. He's no doubt a crook, too. When he makes a play for a bribe or illegal services, I want to get the goods on him. I'll turn him in to his agency and the cops."

"That could take a while, couldn't it?"

"I doubt it. Not with his kind. He's probably making a play to scam someone every day of the week."

Becky listened, but she only felt more confused. Why couldn't he drop it, and concentrate on Lance's recovery? But at the same time, she wanted to help. Becky wanted to soothe the hurt and torment troubling her father's heart. She could wait tables for a few weeks. Her pregnancy wouldn't show for nearly two months. If this IRS agent was as bad as her father suggested, then she might be doing a public service as well.

"Maybe I could do it. If I could get hired for evening work so I wouldn't miss classes, then I could do it. That's when this guy would most likely be there—later in the day, right?

"You can do anything you set your mind to, as smart and pretty as you are, and we both know it." Cleet's smiled and brushed his hand over her hair.

"You could go over there today and apply for a job." Cleet paced the hospital room and talked to the ceiling. "A federal agent shouldn't be in a place like that. He's no doubt squeezing taxpayers, telling them he can do them special favors. I tell you the guy's trash and up to no good. You can flush out what he's up to once you're on the inside."

"What's the name of the place?"

"It's called Sugars. I'm sure they'll hire you, Sweetie, pretty as you are. And you'll make some good money in tips. Thirsty businessmen tip well."

"Sugars." Becky's voice fell as an odd array of images flashed through her mind. That was twice in two minutes her father mentioned her looks.

"Daddy, you said it was a gentleman's club. Does that mean no women go in the place?" An awkward silence hung between them.

"No," Cleet blurted. "that's just a name. There are women there."

"I remember now. I've seen their sign on the street, a silhouette of a topless dancer." Becky walked across the room. "You know full well what a place like that would want me to do, and you were going to let me go in there anyway."

"That's not it at all, Rebecca. They need pretty waitresses, too, and they're not going to ask anyone to dance unless they want to. You said you'd do it, and you won't be there that long. I want that damn agent to pay for his total disregard for the sanctity of our home. If he isn't made to pay, he'll do it to another family. Is that what you want?"

"I can't even think right now. Isn't there some other way? I'm not a performer."

"Rebecca, it's time for you to grow up and quit being so almighty prissy like you can't even touch a frog. We know you're a big girl now, don't we? I pay for your living. I forked out big bucks for you to attend SMU. Junior college wasn't good enough for you. The University of Dallas wasn't good enough for you. When are you going to do your part?"

"Daddy, please." She turned her head against the wall and cried. She remembered the time when he was utterly captivated with her, his first born, his little girl. There was a time when he would never have frowned at her much less raised his voice in her presence. A first-born boy would not have brought him greater happiness. She would crawl into his lap and poke her head under his newspaper, and he would set the paper aside and focus all of his attention on her. She would sit on his knee and grasp a giant finger in each hand, and he would comment to Nancy how their daughter was as beautiful as she.

Becky saw how his gaze now looked right through her. A greater sadness filled her heart because she knew how good a man he really was. Becky wished she could sing him a song of forgiveness that might calm and soothe his broken soul. But for now, he was on a rant. Hate fueled his blood, powered by a wreck of shattered expectations.

Cleet grabbed the phone book from the closet and found the number. "Set an appointment and go apply for a job." He touched her cheek, and she pulled away. "There's nothing to be afraid of. Just do it. It'll be easier than you think."

CHAPTER FIFTEEN

$

BY THE MIDDLE OF THE AFTERNOON, Michael knew he'd had two drinks too many. Elaine had gyrated him out of his cash, and it dawned on him that his girls would be back at the house soon. He drove home slowly and cautiously. The weekend traffic was light. When he got home, the girls had not yet returned from their overnight slumber party.

He brushed his teeth, drank some milk, and popped several sticks of peppermint gum in his mouth. A short time later, a van stopped, and he watched his daughters walk up the drive.

Tonya was into baggy clothes when it wasn't a school day. She wore blue jean overalls, the more pockets the better, and a denim cap. Gretchen wore a white sweater and a knee-length red skirt, her blonde hair braided in pigtails tied with red bows. Michael couldn't deny how much they looked like their mother; light hair and skin with delicate features.

He waited for them in the kitchen. They spent most of their time in the bedroom, but the refrigerator was a regular stop. Michael poured two glasses of milk and found a bag of oatmeal cookies in the pantry.

"Afternoon, girls."

Nine-year-old Gretchen rushed to his side and into his arms. She was more responsive and affectionate when Jan was not around. He picked her up and set her on the counter.

"Hungry?" he asked.

Gretchen nodded and clicked her heels on the lower cabinets.

Tonya saw the milk and cookies, but inspected the refrigerator interior. She made a disagreeable face at what she found, settled on a can of Cheese Whiz, and closed the door.

"Here's some cookies."

"Not now." Eleven-year-old Tonya opened a box of Ritz and proceeded to squirt cheese on a plateful of crackers. Michael poured himself a glass of milk, and the three of them sat at the kitchen table to eat their snacks.

"I thought we could play a board game together," Michael said.

Tonya looked disinterested. Gretchen was two-handing the large glass of milk to her mouth.

"I'll set up the board in the den." He glanced through the selection and settled on Pollyanna and set it up while the girls finished eating. They each selected a color, and he explained the rules.

"I know how to play Pollyanna," Tonya said.

"I know you do, I know. What are you studying in school these days?"

"Multiplication tables," Tonya replied with a thick layer of exasperation.

"You'll be good at it once you learn it."

"I already know how to multiply. Mrs. Wampler keeps going over the same stuff, over and over, for the dumb kids."

Michael didn't know what to say. He turned his attention to Gretchen. "Your turn to roll."

Gretchen rolled a nine and painstakingly moved her piece a space at a time.

"What have you been studying," he asked.

"We read aloud in class."

"That sounds like fun. What about?"

"The Alamo."

They heard a car pull into the garage.

"That's Mom," Tonya said.

"Yes, let's finish our game." Michael rolled the dice.

Jan came through the kitchen with her usual bustle, dropped her briefcase on the floor, and spied the three of them in the den.

"Did you finish that project in the backyard like I asked you? Girls, go to your room."

The girls scampered from the den faster than startled cats, grabbed their backpacks, and were in their bedroom before Michael could say hello.

"We were playing a game."

"Good grief, Michael, after being out all day I'm

sure they have homework to do. You didn't answer my question."

"Maybe I didn't catch it since we were so rudely interrupted."

"You know what I'm talking about, the railing in the back, you promised."

"Yes, I got it all done."

"Well I bet you didn't see this." She opened her briefcase, grabbed a newspaper opened to the Metro section, and marched into the den. She threw it on the card table sending game pieces flying. The headline ran across the top; the story plastered across half of the page.

IRS Agent Shoots Unarmed Teenager

Michael read the headline,. A queasy hollowness rolled in his gut. He pushed the paper aside.

"I wouldn't read it either if I were you," she said. "It's about as incriminating as it can be. Makes you and that uncouth partner of yours come off as uncontrollable goons. Your superiors are really going to appreciate that. At least they didn't mention your name, thank god. I knew the Morning News would run it sooner or later."

"All right, Jan, give it a rest." He stood and walked to the kitchen. When he turned around, she was right there. "You know why I carry a gun. I haven't been dismissed, the boy is recovering, and it would help me if you didn't come across with accusations every time something doesn't fit with your idyllic world."

"You shot somebody. Who is it that's not living

in reality?"

"What's that supposed to mean?"

"You collect taxes. It's a paperwork job for the most part. It's not like you have to bring in violent felons."

"Don't be naive, Jan. I'm assigned to deal with the deadbeats who won't respond to notices from the Service. They're the lowest of the low—money-launderers, blatant tax evaders and career criminals. We have to collect delinquent taxes, and they only respond to a show of force."

She put her hands on her hips. "What category does that teenager fit under?" The room fell silent, and Jan shook her head. "I have to tell you, I have serious misgivings about your job. I thought I would come to accept it because you were inside the IRS. If anything new and important came down the pike, you'd be one of the first to know. But it's not worth the stress it puts me through. If anyone found out my husband shot an unarmed kid in his home, the word-of-mouth gossip would ruin my business."

"I don't want you to worry," he said.

"The story is in the paper, Michael. Your name's not in it, but who's to say it won't come out?"

"Why should anyone find out?"

"Michael, how does anyone find out anything? Just because the paper didn't print your name doesn't mean they don't know who you are. I'm sure the police have your name. I'm very concerned. Your job concerns me. Having a gun in the house concerns me. Keeping my good reputation concerns me. What am I going to do with you?"

Her words made him wince. He wanted some sympathy, some caring respect for the anxiety he'd endured. He wanted to slap her, too, but he would never do that. Maybe that was part of the problem. He had built a family persona of such mundane predictability that the only time he got any attention was when something drastic occurred, and then to get scolded like a toddler.

Michael had had enough. "I'm going out. I need to go back to the office. I'll be back in a few hours."

He got in his Acura and realized he was breathing heavily. He drove through the residential streets of North Dallas to calm down. Maybe it would be different if they had a son. He would be more involved in raising a son. He loved his daughters completely. They were healthy, beautiful, and did well in school. It wasn't his offspring that concerned him.

It was Jan and his marriage. Something had gone wrong. He wanted it to work it out, to grow old with the bright-eyed co-ed he met in college. They were both thirty-three now with careers and two beautiful daughters. Married life should be a partnership of sharing joys and struggles, not a daily gauntlet of bitter words and hurt feelings, Michael thought.

Everything was perfect when they got married six months after they graduated from TCU. He began working for the IRS with his business degree and law enforcement minor. One week they'd take in a rock concert, the next week the Dallas Philharmonic, another week a stage play, and then a comedy club.

Jan got into real estate totally by chance. She found she was good at it and she loved the work. Every house she touched turned into a listing; every family she met turned into a buyer. Michael knew that even with her hectic schedule, she was not under pressure to perform. She was one of the top, if not the top agent at her agency.

Something had changed between him and his wife, and Michael wanted desperately to know how to fix it.

Michael drove into downtown Dallas and parked in a lot two blocks from his office. The federal building was open seven days a week. He used his I.D. card to access the back door and submitted to the cursory, yet mandatory, security screening everyone who entered the building endured every day. It was just past 7:00 P.M.

The pencil-necked auditors on the 5th through 7th floors would still be at work. As bean counters for the federal government, their work never ceased. They worked in two shifts from seven in the morning to eleven at night, six days a week. The Dallas office, along with the IRS complex in Austin handled a five-state region that included Texas, New Mexico, Oklahoma, Arkansas, and Louisiana. Last calendar year the region handled over 20 million, 500 thousand personal and business tax returns. There were a lot of beans to count.

Michael got off the elevator and entered his office area greeted by a few dim lights high in the ceiling that illuminated the walkways. He went to Barnes' office. The door was locked. He wanted to get the Dixon seizure list. If the list were gone,

Barnes wouldn't miss it, at least not for a while. The Dixon's wouldn't be hassled about their personal property. But getting the file would have to wait. Maybe Barnes didn't lock his office during the week.

Michael went to his work area, switched on his computer, and logged onto the IDRS, the Integrated Data Retrieval System. The system held every shred of information on every taxpayer in the region who had ever filed a federal return. Access to the system by revenue officers was restricted to the cases assigned to them. Unauthorized access was grounds for termination.

But accessing information on anyone in Dixon's circle of relatives and business associates was within the guidelines, because their financial affairs may shed light on Dixons's ability, or inability, to pay his taxes. Michael entered Dixon's business EIN for Dixon Metal Fabricators. The tax deficiency was $84,555.10. Michael changed the eight to a three. He looked up two other social security numbers in his caseload, printed off several pages, and logged out.

What he had done could be easily tracked by anyone who compared his password entry to the files accessed. But at the moment, Michael was relieved. Barnes wouldn't be the one to find it. He was too absorbed in collecting money. Barnes had a one track mind to get active cases 'closed' and the files pushed to the left side of his desk. Once the money was collected, it fell into a black hole in Washington.

But the sophisticated algorithms in the computer

programs would eventually track him down. The system matched things up as perfectly as a fine tailor sewing a new suit. If the computer found a payment, it wanted to find a matching bill. And if it found a lower balance on a taxpayer's invoice, it wanted to find the payment that reduced that bill. Before he had taken five steps from the computer console, Michael knew his ploy to change the amount Dixon owed was folly. Changing the numbers on Dixon's tax bill was professional suicide. He sat back down, logged in and changed the amount Dixon owed back to $84,555.10.

CHAPTER SIXTEEN

$

SCHEDULING AN APPOINTMENT to audition as a stripper was as necessary as saying grace over a box of popcorn. Nevertheless, Becky had done so. She made arrangements with a man with a low, raspy voice who couldn't have sounded less interested in her call if she were selling burial plots.

Becky was overwhelmed with emotion as she drove to Sugars. That morning, she had pleaded with her father to dismiss the whole idea, but rather than relent he coached, cajoled, and praised her. She had initially volunteered, he reminded her. There was no good reason not to go through with it. Cleet made outlandish promises which did nothing to increase her motivation. Becky knew all her father wanted was an inside track to Cranfield, a possible way to get dirt on him, and get close enough to hurt him.

Becky parked her Trans Am near the club's back fence. A glance in the rear view mirror revealed bloodshot eyes and tear-streaked cheeks. She reached for more tissues. She looked at the building and shivered. With luck, the management would reject her. With luck, this would all become a distasteful encounter she could soon forget. But, if she didn't get a job, her father would be furious, and he'd come up with another devious scheme that would include her. With Lance getting shot and his money problems, her father had become obsessed with his vendetta. Better to go through with it and hold it all inside for now. It wouldn't last forever.

Once inside, Becky took a moment to let her eyes adjust to the dim interior. The cavernous darkness was illuminated by small aisle lights around the floor perimeter, probably to keep the customers from walking into the walls. Back lighting gleamed through stacks of clean glasses behind the bar. Disco globes painted colored lights around the walls. She approached the first person she saw.

"Hello."

The woman turned and looked her over.

"I'm here to see Omar," Becky said.

"Sure, come with me." They headed to the back. "What's your name?"

"Becky."

"That's a cute name." They entered a lighted hallway through a veil of thick drapes. "My name's Elaine."

Like all exotic dance clubs, Sugars was always interested in new faces, new talent, new bodies. Girls could quit without notice or leave town with someone with a pocket full of cash for a week in Vegas or a day in Shreveport. There were the girls who got too strung out on drugs to work and the ones who called in sick every other day with everything from an inflamed pimple to a case of the clap.

For all the women who applied, only a third of them came close to making the grade. Some of them had worked in the business over the years, but Mother Nature had passed them by, a little too much weight here, a noticeable sag there. Their pleas for one more go-round in the big tent met with deaf ears. Omar didn't run a reclamation farm for old thoroughbreds. He put them out to pasture.

Elaine looked at Becky. Competition for tips and attention at the club was fierce. The last thing the other dancers wanted to compete with was a beauty who would command center stage. Still, Elaine's duties included getting new talent familiar with the routine and policies of the club. "Have you worked at a place like this before?"

Becky shook her head.

Elaine smiled. "That's okay. You'll do just fine. The customers aren't allowed to touch you. It's really easy. I'll be here to help you. Would you like that?"

Becky swallowed and nodded.

Elaine brushed her fingers over Becky's cheek. "You'll do just fine," Elaine repeated. She rapped on a door, and when a voice grumbled from inside, she opened it.

"This is Becky."

Omar grunted, beckoned with his fingers, and pushed away from a file drawer. A transplanted Pakistani who grew up in Toronto, Omar Ahuja was all about making money and making it as easily as possible. He was burly, blustery, and bald.

"Becky, huh?"

Elaine left them alone.

"Yes."

"Well, come over here, girl. Omar stood and looked her over. Becky's stride was both athletic and elegant. She was slim yet shapely, endowed yet symmetrical. Her presence commanded attention. Omar's eyes lit up, and he quickly forgot what he'd been doing.

"So you want to be an exotic dancer?"

"Yes." Her tone lacked all conviction.

"Well, listen. There's good money to be made here for someone like you. We can teach you all you need to know. You be nice to the customers, they'll be nice to you. The way it works is the house gets all the money from drinks, and you get to keep all of your tips. There's a shift fee the dancers pay, but we'll waive that for you until you learn the ropes. Ever danced seductively on stage and let the colored lights bounce off your bare tits?"

Becky recoiled as though she'd been punched. "No."

"That's okay. We'll work you through it. Like I said, we'll teach you everything you need to know. Take off your jacket and turn around."

Becky dropped her gaze and complied. She held

the windbreaker in both hands as she turned in a tight circle.

"Relax. All we do is entertain people, Sweetheart," Omar said. "It's all a show, nothing serious. Just relax. Take a deep breath."

Becky did. Her brown eyes appeared as pools of melted chocolate. Omar was impressed. "Walk over to that desk and back." Omar didn't care in the least why she decided to come in for a job. He was just glad she had. He wanted her to settle down long enough to give it a chance. Usually, he'd ask her to take off her top under the pretense of qualifying her physical attributes. It was a free show for him. But he didn't want to push his luck with this rookie beauty. Better to take it slow.

"Can I be a waitress?"

"For starters, I suppose. We'll work you in slow."

"I don't know. I don't think I can get on stage and dance for strangers like you want me to." The last few minutes had turned her body into a bundle of nerves, and her mind full of doubt.

"That's where the money is, Sweetheart."

"I should probably go. I'm sorry."

"No, now wait a minute. You're having beginners jitters. All the girls feel nervous at first. We'll do it your way, okay? You can wait tables, how's that? Get the hang of things."

Becky nodded and put her windbreaker back on.

"When can you start?"

Becky shrugged slightly. "Anytime, I guess."

Omar smiled, his thick puffy lips stretched like a rubber band. "How about this afternoon? Say at five o'clock?"

"Okay, I can come back then."

"Go see Elaine now and she'll find you some outfits to wear and explain how things work."

"I'll do my best."

"Good," Omar said. "Now give me a big smile."

Becky looked delicious, even with the forced effort of her upturned lips. Omar chuckled to himself as Becky left the office.

CHAPTER SEVENTEEN

$

MONDAY MORNING, Barnes called Michael and Frank into his office. Barnes collar, for the moment, was still buttoned. His faded brown tie was still in place. All of that would change soon enough. Before long, his sleeves would be rolled up past his elbows with a loosened tie dangling from his neck.

"Have a seat," Barnes said as he stood behind his huge mahogany desk, spread his arms wide and leaned over it. "Couple of things—the boys in Internal Investigations are collecting overtime getting to the bottom of your 'warning shot.' They'll come up with sufficient provocation for drawing your weapon. As for firing it, sure would have been better if you'd shot the old man instead of the kid."

Barnes took in a deep breath. "I'm doing my best to cover your ass, Cranfield, so you better make it worth my time." He starred at Michael and screwed his face up in disdain. "This Mr. Dixon has a large responsibility in all of this. He's trying to make a stink with the cops and the press, but I'm not playing his game. If he'd behaved like a rational adult none of this would have happened. Right?"

Barnes glanced at Frank, who nodded in agreement. Michael remained silent.

"I got word over the weekend the kid went back into surgery, so this is going to be with us for a while. The doctors didn't stitch him up right the first time. In the meantime, we still have this file."

Barnes reached for a file labeled Dixon Metal Fabricators.

Michael swallowed. He wanted to think about other things. He didn't need Dixon pushed back in his face first thing Monday morning. He shot a glance at Frank and saw him nodding slightly, a smirk curled at the edges of his mouth.

"The U.S. Treasury is expecting the back assessments owed by Dixon," Barnes continued. "The file is yours now. Edwards has been given other assignments." Barnes thrust the paperwork at Michael. "I have half a mind to send a van over to his house right now, and confiscate the items on that list. But I'm not going to do it. Not now, anyway. I'm not giving Dixon additional ammunition for his tirades to the press." Barnes yanked his chair forward and dropped his backside into the seat.

"What I want from you two is to seize both his personal and business bank accounts. I want the funds from those accounts. Get the cashier's checks from the bank manager in payment toward Dixon's tax deficiency. I'll consider what to do next after I see how much he has in the bank and the boy is out of the hospital. Any questions?"

Michael stepped forward and dropped the file on the front edge of Barnes' desk. "Come on, boss. Both accounts? The guy has a business to run. The guy has over thirty employees and regular customers. It'll ruin him to shut down his business for even a week."

Barnes glared. Michael could see muscles tighten in his jaw. After a few moments, Barnes relaxed a bit and pointed at the chair in front of his desk. "Take a seat, Cranfield." Frank remained standing and stepped back. Barnes leaned forward and folded his hands together.

"I've had high-paid lawyers, accountants, and business owners sitting right where you are," Barnes said, "singing their sad songs of doom and gloom if their clients or their businesses don't get a little more time to pay Uncle Sam what they owe. Their sob stories are so pitiful they would make pro wrestlers weep. But you're the first—the first time I've ever had a federal agent try to feed me that crap. You knew you had to put on your big boy pants when you took this job. Why you getting soft, Cranfield?"

"I'll collect the money, boss. I'll stay on it until it's paid. Just don't close him down. That's not going to benefit anyone in the long run. Besides, Dixon's been paying the correct tax on his business income. It's an irregularity in the social security contributions for his employees that's created this problem. I've looked at everything in the file. Maybe it's just an oversight. Dixon's father ran the business until his recent death. I'm telling you the guy needs to get organized with his new responsibilities and he'll be square."

Barnes sat dumbfounded. He glanced at Frank, then rubbed his upper lip and cleared his throat. "Well jeez, Cranfield. That was a nice little speech." Barnes tone was commending. "Considering Dixon would probably squash you like a bug if he could, he'll never know you went to bat for him. But we have to collect taxes. Go close out his personal bank account. We'll go with that for now."

Before Michael could say another word, Frank grabbed him by the arm and pulled him from the room. We'll get it done," Frank said. "We'll take care of it."

****

Once at the bank, Michael and Frank would be in and out in no time. With their IRS credentials seizing bank accounts was easier than snatching purses from old ladies. Michael and Frank flashed their badges and moved swiftly through the bank's layered chain of command. Within minutes, they stood in the office of an executive vice president.

"How can I help you, gentlemen?" Michael took a good look at the banker. The guy probably had his hair trimmed twice a week. His button-down white collar and gold tie chain accentuated a professional appearance designed to impress and intimidate. His black shoes absolutely gleamed. Michael looked at his shoes. He couldn't remember the last time he'd polished them. He had to admit, the bank officer had a prestigious position, and was probably well paid. But he would never have a fraction of the power over the lives of people he and Frank possessed. And all they had to do was shine their badges every now and again.

"Need to get all of the funds from an account with a cashier's check made out to the Service," Michael said as he gave the man the account number.

In seconds it was done. The balance in the account amounted to $7,227.00. Not a great sum. It would hardly make a dent in the deficiency judgment Dixon owed the federal treasury. That wasn't the point. Confiscating the funds would refocus Dixon's attention. Closing the account would reaffirm Uncle Sam still expected to be paid.

As they walked from the bank, Michael could no longer keep quiet. "I don't like doing this when a man is down. I mean, what's the rush? Dixon has a business to run and a kid in the hospital. He certainly isn't going anywhere, not when his debts are a fraction of his assets. He's just strapped for cash right now."

Frank listened. Everyone was entitled to their opinion, at least theoretically. But you wouldn't hear any complaints about the Service coming from Frank. His spiel was always the company line. He had too many skeletons buried to cause anyone to start digging.

"Hey, before we head out, let me buy you a cup of coffee," Frank said. "There's a place up another block where I catch lunch every once in a while."

It was nearly 10:30 when the men walked into the Golden Cue. The place was a musty, smokey downtown hangout walled off from the next door warehouse. Ceiling fans hummed in the rafters while an overworked window air conditioner groaned in the back. Cuss words stabbed the din of muffled conversations. Dominoes smacked against Masonite game tables with a crack, the sound of a bull whip. At noon each weekday, an influx of the starch-collared crowd from surrounding offices would invade the place for a bowl of Deacon's homemade chili or a lunch-hour game of pool.

The Golden Cue was a retiree hangout. Men began congregating around eight because their wives wanted them up and out of the house. For others, the attraction of the Cue was just the opposite. It served as a change of scenery from the surroundings at home, and provided someone else to talk to besides the strange old woman who lived in their house.

A few able-bodied men were sprinkled among the regulars. They drifted in and out, passed out hot tips on horses that ran at Lone Star Park, and hustled games of pool for a few bucks or a pack of smokes. Occasionally, a street weary wino would saunter in and attempt to catch a few Z's on the bench seats that lined the walls. But Deacon, the owner, would promptly jerk them up, cuss them out, and hustle them out the back. The Cue might be a classless hole-in-the-wall pool hall with worn through linoleum floors and cobwebs in the corners, but it was for paying customers only.

"Morning, Deacon, two coffees," Frank said, as he and Michael staked out a wobbly malt shop table next to a silent jukebox. A cue ball cracked against a rack of billiard balls. The place was getting livelier as the morning wore on, and the beverage of choice made the slow transition from coffee to beer.

Frank held five sugar packets together, ripped them open, and shook them into his coffee. He stirred the coffee with a stick and looked around. No one was near enough to overhear them. "I can't believe you got out of Barnes' office without your walking papers. I swear, it blows my mind he took your backtalk. You better tread lightly, my friend. Barnes might have been in a good mood this morning, but he won't be so forgiving you try that again." Frank took a sip of coffee, his gaze focused straight at Michael. "You're going to have to shake it off."

"I can't get my mind off of last week. It wasn't like I shot a guy holding a shotgun. Being responsible for shooting that kid. It's hard to get any sleep after something like that." Michael scooted forward in his chair and took a deep breath. "I know we have to collect revenue, but you know Dixon is counting on that money we froze. After we showed up last week, he knows the Service is serious. Couldn't further collection activity wait for a week or two?"

"So you don't mind what we do. It's Dixon and the boy that's got you all bent out of shape?"

"I'm beginning to question it all, Frank. I know

the government has to collect taxes, but maybe there's a better way to go about it. And still, once it gets to Washington, they can't keep track of all the money if their lives depended upon it. They waste half of what they get, and a good amount of what they do spend disappears in the form of corporate welfare and subsidies to people who are perfectly capable of taking care of themselves."

"It's politics," Frank offered.

"I know, but this country wasn't built on handouts. Everyone says they want the government to leave them alone, but they stick their hands in the government cookie jar every chance they get."

"I suppose that's why politicians do it—to get the public beholden to them," Frank said. "But you still have a job to do. Nothing we can do about Washington. Nothing we can do."

"To hell with Washington." Michael's voice rose for an instant, but he immediately brought it back down. "That's not what bothers me. I'd like to know why we have to strong arm all of these people. I'm getting tired of the crap."

Frank's gaze zeroed in on his partner. "Because they won't pay if we don't, and you know it."

Michael leaned back and stared at the fifteen-foot ceiling. Now it was Frank's turn to lean across the table.

"You're a big boy, Cranfield. Don't act so naive. You don't have to be Ivy League to be an intellectual snob in the grand ole USA. This country is teeming with semi-educated, semi-literate do gooders whose sole purpose in life is to help the down-trodden and destitute.

"As time passes, by the good fortune of health and decent jobs, they get in a position where their lives are fairly secure. They join the PTA or the Rotary Club, get advanced university degrees or serve on the school board or some highfalutin committee, and before long they know what's best for everyone else.

"They give to their church and send a hundred dollars to the Heart Association, but to get anything significant accomplished, they jump into Uncle Sam's deep pockets with all the good intentions of saving the world. Hell, every non-profit out there thinks their mission is so noble they shouldn't have to raise a dime—Uncle Sam should foot the bill for all their worthy efforts.

"To save the world, all these projects need big money. The politicians who can fund their noble causes need votes. To perpetuate this cycle of symbiotic benevolence, they all jump into bed together and circle jerk the federal treasury in the best interests of the common man.

"So we, meaning you and me, do what we do. If one evening some small businessman puts a bullet through his brain because he can't pay his back taxes or can't stand the shame of facing his family because of it, don't think for one minute that Helen Housewife from Springfield who founded a battered women's shelter with the help of a federal grant is going to see any connection to her."

Frank threw down the last of his coffee. "But what the hell do I know? You're right about one thing, Cranfield. It's all about the money. If you don't like the rules, run for Congress." Frank took a deep breath and spat the splintered remains of his swizzle stick into the cup.

"Now you've got me all worked up." Frank threw four bucks on the table. "Let's get Dixon's check to the office. We have to go by several businesses in Arlington before the day is over. The sooner the better as far as I'm concerned."

CHAPTER EIGHTEEN

$

CLEET FINALLY RETURNED HOME. Lance's long-term prognosis filled his brain with tortured images. He figured Lance would live, but that was hardly a consoling thought. What if he had to buy his boy a wheelchair to use for the rest of his life? The possibility brought waves of mental anguish.

His mind was at the point where the coercion of his daughter to get a job at a strip club seemed like a reasonable request. He would make IRS Special Agent Cranfield pay, but first, he would make him suffer. Becky could surely find something incriminating on a married man who frequented strip clubs. She could find something he could use to wreck the man's marriage or get him fired from his comfortable government job. When Cleet finally fell into bed, he slept until noon the next day.

After he was up and dressed, Cleet remembered something else that had been scratching in the corner of his brain. He knew the company had been receiving notices from the IRS for months. He thought Dorothy had taken care of it. She handled payroll, deductions for worker's share of medical premiums, sick leave credit, and vacation time. Dorothy was a one-woman Human Resources department. She worked with the company's accountant whom Cleet had never met. The accountant had been hired by his father long before Cleet joined the company. Now his thoughts focused on how Dorothy and this accountant had put him in such a bind.

Cleet called Dorothy at her home on a Sunday afternoon.

"Listen, Dorothy, I was a nervous wreck about Lance when I was at the office. I forgot to ask you a few things."

"Certainly, sir."

"When those IRS agents came pushing their way into my house, well, a lot of things slipped my mind."

"I can understand that," Dorothy said.

"So, Dorothy, you saw the notices from the IRS that came to the office? I gave them to you, I remember. They said we were short employee social security contributions. It wasn't a large amount at the time. It's grown to over $80,000. That's why those agents were at my door. Why didn't you take care of that? I expected you to do so. You said you would."

A pause lingered in the line. "Well, Mr. Dixon. The fact is—I thought I did. I faxed the notices over to the accountant and told him to increase the total quarterly company social security contributions to whatever was needed to get them caught up within six months. He said he would take care of it. I think I talked to him several different times about the matter, and every time he said he had it taken care of."

For a moment, Cleet gazed through the glass patio door into the backyard. An IRS agent had injured his son, but his inept accountant seemingly caused his tax problems in the first place. He realized there were many things he didn't know about the business his father had started almost thirty years ago. He had been working as a sales manager for a ready-mix concrete company when his father died. He tried to get up to speed taking over an entirely different kind of company, but there was so much to learn about Dixon Metal Fabricators..

"Has anything like this happened before with this guy?"

"Not as long as I've been with the company, Mr. Dixon.

"So, who is he?"

"His name is Bill Raney."

Bright and early Monday morning, Cleet sat in his car across the parking lot from Raney's office. It was nine, and no one had shown. Cleet walked down several doors to a Starbucks and sipped an expresso. At 9:45, Cleet went back and found

Raney's door open.

The front area had a couch, a coffee table with a few magazines scattered across it, and a desk with no one there. "Good morning," Cleet announced as the door closed behind him.

A slender man, well into his sixties, poked his head out from a back office. His steps were slow as he approached the front. The skin on his face was as translucent as cellophane. "May I help you?"

"Yes. I wanted to discuss some business, Mr. Raney."

"I'm sorry," Raney said. "I'm terribly busy this morning. You should have called for an appointment."

Cleet motioned toward the empty front desk. "Your secretary out sick today?"

Raney ignored the comment. "Would you like to make an appointment?"

A wide grin erupted on Cleet's face. "I don't need an appointment, Bill. The name's Dixon. Dixon Metal Fabricators and you've got some explaining to do." Cleet was twice Raney's size and placed his hand on the man's shoulder and turned him toward the back office.

"Look, I don't know what you're thinking, but I don't want no trouble." If there had been any blood in Raney's sallow cheeks, it was gone.

"Oh, you're way past trouble, Bill." Cleet pushed him into the office and closed the door. "My office manager tells me you knew we were getting notices from the IRS, and you did nothing to resolve the problem." Cleet pulled a chair up to Raney's desk. "Go ahead. Sit down, Bill. We're going to be here a while until I get some answers."

Raney slipped behind his desk. Once seated, Cleet leaned back in his chair, lifted his leg, and dropped his heel on the front of the desk with a bang. Raney sat stiff as a board. "Now I know you had plenty of money on hand since you make our quarterly business estimated tax payments, and keep the books on our business expenses and sales. So, not taking care of outstanding tax bills tells me you either cooked our returns for your benefit or are skimming company money off the top, or both."

"I swear, it's nothing like that."

"I can tell you're lying. You're already sweating. I can see it." Cleet pulled his foot off the desk and scooted his chair closer. "Did you know my son got shot when agents came to my house?"

"That was your boy? I read about it. I'm so sorry."

"Sorry, my ass. How would you like it if I took that computer keyboard and rammed it down your miserable throat?"

"Please, I don't want no trouble."

"I should have come in sooner, but I've got a pretty good idea as to what you've got going on here." Cleet leaned over the desk. "You've been in business for a long time. You've got customers from way back who let you handle their accounting and don't ask questions. My father trusted you somewhere along the line, but I say, you're nothing but a crook.

"I'm going to have my company books audited by an outside group. If you've been embezzling, I'll have you thrown in jail. As of now, you're fired! I want all my ledgers, disks, and all the info on the computer—NOW. Don't leave anything out or I'll be back. And you don't want me to come back."

Cleet paced the room as Raney worked feverishly at the computer. When Raney finished, he handed everything to Cleet, including a business checkbook. Cleet stepped in Raney's space and blew his breath in older man's face.

"One other thing, Bill. You're not getting off that easy. The IRS wants $80,000 from me and you're going to find it and remit it. We both know you have other well-off clients. They won't mind contributing to the cause. One way or the other, find the money, or I'll pull it from your hide with a pair of pliers. I have nothing to lose. You have thirty days." With that, Cleet pushed Raney into his desk chair, took the ledgers and computer disks, and left.

CHAPTER NINETEEN

$

MICHAEL AND FRANK made three stops in Arlington. All the time, Michael thought of ways to ease the pressure on the Dixon family. What he was contemplating would likely be discovered, and he'd lose his job. But that possibility was secondary. It might be for the best. The duties of the job were getting to him. His health and sanity were more important than a job with the federal government.

When he and Frank returned to Dallas, Michael ate supper by himself at a diner near Baylor Medical Center. It wasn't yet six. He needed to wait until at least seven to go back to the office when he could be fairly certain everyone who worked on his floor would be gone. He thought of going to Sugars to kill some time but decided against it. Not tonight.

A few minutes past seven Michael passed through the security checkpoints of the federal building and took the elevator to his floor. He was the only one there. He tried Barnes door. Again it was locked. He went back into the hallway and found the janitor cleaning a women's bathroom.

"Hey, buddy," Michael said, "you got a key so I can get into my office?"

The janitor was young, tall and lanky. He stopped what he was doing and gave Michael the once over. His gaze was intelligent and expressive. Michael could tell the young man was destined for more than cleaning toilets all his life. "Can I see your ID?" the young man asked.

Michael flipped out his badge "It's just across the hall. Won't take a minute."

"This says Barnes," the young man said, pointing to the nameplate when they got to the office door.

"Yeah, my supervisor. Need one file that has to be worked tonight."

The young man eyed Michael closely. "Sorry. If it isn't your office, I can't open it."

Michael rubbed his chin. "I understand. But your help would be a big time saver."

The young man shook his head. "Before I got this job I listened for two weeks to my boss spout off all the regulations about working here before I even set foot in this building. If I let you in that room, I'll lose my job for sure."

"No one will ever know I was in there," Michael said. "All my boss cares about is closed cases. If the file isn't in there, he'll never miss it."

"But if he does, I'd be the first person to be questioned. Can't do it."

"Come with me for a minute." Michael led the janitor into the hall and back down to the bathroom he was cleaning. Listen," he said. "I'll level with you. A few days ago I was serving a property seizure and things got out of hand. I drew my handgun, and a teenage boy got shot by accident. I want to get that file so the family doesn't lose a lot of personal property that won't make a dent in what they owe the government. I know it'll be sold for pennies on the dollar. But if they don't lose that property, it might give them some peace right now."

The young man kept his wide, expressive eyes on Michael and listened to every word. They looked at each other in silence.

Finally, Michael spoke. "Would you do that for a family in turmoil? Or does that stare of yours mean you want to shake me down? The tall fellow stood right where he was, but Michael knew he was listening—he was thinking, but remained silent..

"I give you money and you accept it, that's a bribe and a felony for both of us. We don't want to go down that road. However, if you want to help out a family you don't know by opening that door, it's just between you and me, and their lives will be a little easier for the time being, at least."

The young man's face relaxed. "Listen, mister, I believe you. You seem like a nice guy and I know you've got a tough job. But I can't open that door for you, and really, you don't want me to. It would only make things worse in the long run.

Slowly, Michael nodded. "Yeah, you're right,"

he said. He headed for the door, then turned back. "Just between you and me?"

"Sure.," the young man said. "Just between you and me."

****

When Becky returned to Sugars for her first shift, the apprehension that churned in her body made her nauseous. She parked her Trans Am in the back lot by the fence and slipped from the car wearing a scarf and sunglasses. She knocked on the employees' entrance nestled between two giant hedges

"I'm here to see Elaine. I'm a new waitress."

"She's here," hollered the buxom blonde who answered the door, as she looked Becky over. "We usually keep this door locked. You can come in the front, you know."

Becky let her eyes adjust to the shadowy interior, then took a few steps down a hall and looked into the main room. It was happy hour, and the club was a churning mass of humanity. Pungent smoke swirled in the air. The music drifted with seductive strings; the melody hypnotic and erotic.

"Right on time." Elaine smiled and led her behind the bar. "This is Kevin. He's the barback." The young man smiled and continued stacking glasses. "That's Lana and that's Sasha." Both were busy pouring drinks. "Follow me." Elaine led Becky back of the main stage to a wardrobe closet next to a communal dressing room. They passed several semi-naked girls, chain-smoking and cussing as they got ready to go on stage. The room glittered and shimmered with sequins and satin. The girls gave Becky the once over as she walked by.

"Let's try on some of these outfits while we have the time," Elaine said. She handed Becky a sleeveless royal blue blouse with long tails to be tied in front under the breasts. Radiant red pants that billowed like a flag in the breeze went with the blouse. The final touch, white gloves and bow tie had Becky looking like Uncle Sam ready to lead troops to an orgy.

"You look gorgeous," Elaine beamed. "Sit down and let's talk. First of all, you need a name while in the club, a stage name. These guys will often ask who you are. You don't want to be giving out your real name. Some of them will come onto you like they want to be your sugar daddy, and try to convince you if you hook up with them, you'll never have another care in the world. Boy, do I wish I had a nickel for every time I've heard that one.

"Others will ask you out on a date. Most of them are married, but not all. They have good jobs and make good money, but they're either bored with what they got at home or the ole lady cut them off. Some of them will tip like they inherited a fortune, but they're as quiet as church mice. They think you're supposed to read their minds and know how they feel. Don't get caught up in none of that shit. You're here to entertain, not become a psychologist."

Becky swallowed and listened. It seemed like Elaine was trying to help her, not have her thrown to the wolves. "Thanks. This is all new to me."

"No problem. I was a beginner once. Thought of a name?"

"Not really. What do the other girls use?"

"Oh, let's see. We've got an Angel and a Francine, a Misty, and an Amber. It doesn't matter as long as it isn't your real name."

"Why did you choose Elaine?"

"My real name is Ruth." Elaine scrunched up her nose. "Not a real sexy handle. Anyway, I got an aunt named Elaine, and she's a classy lady, so that's what I chose."

"I really don't know."

"Okay, let's see. How about Crystal?"

"That's fine," Becky said.

"From now on you're Crystal around here. That's how I'll introduce you to the girls. That's what you tell the swinging dicks."

"I beg your pardon?"

"The customers. I'll help you out, but don't be a prude. These guys are in here to look at your body. Every one of them would take you to bed if you'd let them."

Becky shuddered.

"That's why you smile at them and take their money, and that's it. Don't get involved with these guys. If they were interested in a serious relationship, they'd be in church." Elaine raised her arm and rotated her hand. "Stand up and move in a circle. Just think about the music, slow, nice, and easy. The guys want to see you move in front of them."

"But Omar said I could just serve drinks."

"Yeah, I know. This is for practice if you want to

dance later on. Besides, there's no money in waiting tables. You want to make some money, right? And anyway, you think dancing's difficult or embarrassing. There's nothing to it once you've done it a time or two. Let me talk you through it once, okay?"

Becky took a deep breath and nodded.

"Remember, listen to the music and look down at the edge of the stage. After you've moved up and down the stage, pull the knot on the blouse, let it slide off one arm, it will fall off your back, then drop your other arm and let it drop to the floor."

Becky kept moving as Elaine coached. A sense of shame rose within Becky even though she was dancing in front of a woman and other girls who turned to watch.

"Bend over, look through your legs, make eye contact, and smile. Whenever you see money flapping ease yourself to the front of the stage, kneel, and let them put the money in your waistband or garter. Repeat your steps before you take off another piece of clothing."

"Now with the bra. The snaps are always in front. Go ahead; unsnap it."

Becky complied, and the bra fell open.

"Let it fall to the floor or toss it aside. Very good."

Becky stood topless. She didn't try to cover herself, but she hunched her shoulders with her arms held closely to her sides.

"Relax, everything will fall into place," Elaine said. "All these customers are doing is looking. You can make four or five hundred dollars a night, a thousand on weekends. Modesty don't pay that kind of money. You don't need to do any more today."

"Let's get you into a cocktail dress so you can wait tables." Elaine pulled out a pink one-piece, thigh-high dress with frilly straps and handed it to Becky. Once she had it on, Elaine handed her a tiny white apron.

"Thanks, Elaine, for taking the extra time with me."

"No problem. Let's go to the bar. You'll work under Lana. She'll assign you some tables to work."

Lana gave Becky a cursory nod when reintroduced. In addition to her pushed up breasts which needed extra support because of their size, certainly not to enhance them, Lana sported enough eyeliner to shame a raccoon. She was an old hand at pouring drinks. Tending bar was a job, pure and simple, and Lana could just as easily been laying bricks.

"Here's a tray and a stack of coasters. Pop one of these down in front of a customer and ask them what you can get them to drink. Beer's two dollars in cans until seven when happy hour ends. No draft, no bottles. Well drinks are three-fifty, that's the cheap stuff, and premium liquor is five bucks. Try to keep it simple, bourbon and coke, gin and tonic. Take those three tables along the wall. See, two guys just sat down."

Becky took a deep breath and made her way to the table. Luck was with her. All they wanted was beer. Patrons continued to crowd into the club as the rabble rose in volume. In spite of the loud music and swirl of colored lights, time in the artificial world moved at a slower pace. Becky found herself becoming more at ease. She caught herself smiling. She graciously accepted the tips offered.

"Becky, Becky, is that you?"

Reflexively, she turned to the table behind her. Horror overtook her expression as recognition filled her eyes. She came face-to-face with Matt's dumbstruck, quizzical, wide-eyed look. He was having a beer with two buddies and taking in the scenery of exposed female flesh. His expression quickly morphed from shock to loathing.

"What are you doing here?"

She couldn't speak. She had no defense, certainly nothing Matt would understand. Instantly she knew anything she said would dig her a deeper hole.

"I might ask you the same thing."

"I'm just having a beer."

"Don't let him kid you, Sugarplum," piped up one of his friends. "He knows his way around this place better than the campus library."

"Shut up."

"So, you come in here a lot?" She could think of nothing better to say.

"I've been in here some, so what? Why are you waiting tables? You dancing too?"

"It's not what you think."

"Boy, you sure had me fooled, and to think I lost sleep worrying about you."

"No, Matt. Don't say that. I can explain."

"I know you don't have to work. Did you quit school? You're probably not carrying my baby either, are you? Could be anyone's. Boy, you had me going."

"Let me talk to you later, please. Matt, I can explain everything."

"I can see all the explanation I need. Come on, let's go. I think I'm going to get sick if I don't get out of here."

"Hey, I just opened this one."

"Leave it. I'll get you another."

Becky watched the three young men walk out. She was struck catatonic by his false insinuations and could neither scream or cry though her brain wanted to do both. She stood bewildered and stared at the club entrance until a tap on her shoulder pulled her from her trance.

"Hey, little lady, could you get me another beer?"

CHAPTER TWENTY

$

THE NEXT DAY AT THE OFFICE, Michael completed paperwork from the previous day and left with Frank on another "visit." They would either collect the full delinquency tax owed or shut down another taxpayer's business.

When Michael first joined the service he was assigned the position of Revenue Officer. After a few years, his proficiency was rewarded with advancement to the more prestigious Special Agent. But he never lost his 'collection' mentality. When the Dallas Police Department became unwilling to assist with collection activities due to both a shortage of manpower and unfavorable press after a botched IRS raid, the Service had to send armed Special Agents to assist with seizures and collection of seriously delinquent accounts.

Most Special Agents preferred to work with U.S. attorneys investigating tax schemes or organized crime. But Michael volunteered for the collection assignments. That's where he'd made his name, and until last week, he enjoyed being law enforcement muscle on collection calls. Frank went wherever duty called. He was an old hand in the Service. As long as he kept busy, Frank was happy. For five years Michael took all assignments in stride. But today, as he and Frank drove from the federal building, Michael questioned it all.

Frank did all the talking at their first stop. He flashed his badge at the taxpayer like a beam of light and told him in a measured voice, yet threatening terms, his business was about to be padlocked if he didn't pay. Michael felt sorry for a total stranger. When they left the business, Frank had his usual erect posture and a glint of amusement on his face. Michael said nothing.

The IRS, like all federal agencies, was too big for one person to affect negatively. No matter how many people cheated, absconded, or downright evaded their tax obligations, the department kept rolling along. With well over 100,000 employees, it was a never-ending, unstoppable paper pushing machine. Michael wanted to help the Dixon's out of their tax dilemma, but now he wanted to help others too. That afternoon before he left the office, Michael pulled the last ten cases where he and Frank had padlocked a business and took the business names and addresses with him when he left the building.

After he and Frank completed their rounds for

the day, Michael drove straight to Sugars. Maybe a change of scenery would pull him from his mental funk. He thought about Jan and the fact they hadn't spoken two words to each other in several days. She was gone and had taken the girls to school by the time he got up. He hardly saw her in the evenings either. She would mentally crucify him if he lost his job and the federal benefits that came with them.

Was Jan having an affair? He knew she was a top producer and her workload was real. Whenever he called her office, Jan was there or on an appointment. But who's to say she wasn't showing houses to a secret lover with whom she could knock out twenty minutes of fun on the carpeted floor in an empty house? The idea ate at his skull. She had once been so agreeable, so available, so loving. He didn't buy the notion that two children and a career automatically brought all of that to a halt.

The moment he entered Sugars, Michael was in a better mood. The music, the voices, the lights, and the bare flesh was a balm to his psyche. He sat at a table in the far corner and ordered a margarita. He didn't take a close look at the waitress who served his drink, but the waitress noticed him.

"Can I get you some peanuts or pretzels?" Becky asked when she returned with his drink.

"Sure. Some peanuts would be great."

When she returned, Michael asked, "Is Elaine around?"

"No. She doesn't come in until six, but I can keep you company if you like."

Michael took a slug of his drink and glanced at her face, but he couldn't see much in the shadows of the room. "Sure. Why not?"

"Can I get you another drink?"

"Sure, and get yourself one too. Here's forty."

"I'll be right back." Becky went to Byron's observation post behind the DJ booth. "This guy gave me forty if I'd sit and talk with him."

"Fine by me," Byron said. "You're not on the rotation, so you owe the house half." He extended his hand, and she gave him a twenty. "Tell Lana you're off the tables for a while and take off your apron."

Becky went and got drinks and returned to Michael, who seemed to be staring at the ceiling.

"Here we are," she said, as she sat beside him so he couldn't look directly at her face.

Michael took a hefty swig of his margarita and placed his elbows on the table. "Did you ever get so sick of work you were ready to throw it all away?"

"I think everyone has at one time or another," Becky said.

"Yeah, everybody at some time or another," Michael said, the words coated in defeat.

"Everything can't be so bad. You have friends, co-workers, someone at home." Becky was prying. Michael's emotions were at low tide. If she were to find out anything scandalous, it might be now.

Michael rolled the cold glass between his hands. "Well, I have two beautiful little girls. My wife—well, my wife. She's a good person. She's a good mother." His voice faded off.

"And business is good. It could be better, but it's good?" Becky prompted.

"I only wish I had a business. No, I work for a salary. A good ole government soldier. Great benefits but that's about all. Hound the public, kick some ass. Make believe you're above it all."

"You make it sound frightening. What is it you do?"

"I can't get into that. What did you say your name was?"

"I'm Crystal."

"Thanks for listening, Crystal." Michael finished his drink. "I have to go. I'm not going to wait around until six to see Elaine. Maybe another day."

****

Jan Cranfield awoke at 6:30, and began preparations for a busy day of listing appointments, showings, and an open house. She glanced at Michael deep in dreamland. By the time he got up, she and the girls would have had breakfast and be long gone. But she needed him home by five tonight when the girls expected supper. An open house that began at three might easily run late. She left Michael a note.

At the office, Jan assembled the particulars on three homes she planned to show a couple named Fetter. The buyers arrived late for their 9:00 appointment and it was after ten when they left the first house. She had a listing appointment at 11:30. She was not a person to be late — time to put her sales skills into high gear.

The Fetters could play with the bathroom fixtures and rub the dining room Berber carpet to their heart's content—but later. Right now, she wanted them to fall in love with one of her selected homes. They were going to buy anyway, and quickly. They had moved from Houston and he was already working at his new job. They were living in an apartment with all their possessions in storage.

Jan knew how to play every prospect and lay on the charm. If the prospects were dry, introverts without an ounce of personality, Jan became as stoic as a monk attending to the slightest detail. If the opposite were true, like the Fetters, Jan became one of the family. Jan became as warm and outgoing as the situation required.

But Jan didn't waste time. She made sure sellers were serious and realistic about their asking price. She qualified buyers concerning credit and income with the detail of a bank auditor. An hour later, Jan had the Fetters ready to make an offer. Jan had her executive secretary Liz handle the paperwork. Jan headed to her listing appointment with twenty minutes to spare.

The listing appointment was equally successful. Jan ate a leisurely lunch of chicken salad and coffee at Panera's and returned a few phone calls. She returned to the office, reviewed the Fetter offer Liz had completed and took it to the listing agent's office. By the time she got to the open house, it was almost three.

Liz already had the front door open. Liz was a conscientious executive secretary, a great person to have around. Jan had listed this house a week ago, and she thought for sure it wouldn't last past one open house. The drive-up appeal was impressive.

Manicured hedges lined the front separating the house from the sidewalk. Window planter boxes bloomed with flowers and mature elm trees adorned the front yard.

Liz had an assortment of cookies arranged on a tray. Cups set on the kitchen counter with a fresh pot of coffee brewing. A guest book was open on a stand beside the front door.

"My, I thought I'd get here first, but you've got everything ready to go," Jan said as she sat her satchel on the floor.

"Just wanted to make sure everything was ready in case you ran late," Liz replied.

"I'm glad you did." And without another word, Jan walked across the floor, gently guided Liz to the enclosed laundry area beyond the kitchen, and placed a long wet kiss upon her lips.

CHAPTER TWENTY-ONE

$

IT WAS SEVERAL DAYS before Michael made it back to Sugars. Barnes had gotten another burr up his butt and doubled the workload on his agents. The overdue caseload was growing rather than diminishing. Barnes wouldn't have it. A maze of individuals endured Michael and Frank's dire speeches, day after day. Michael was exhausted.

Word had it the Dixon boy was still in the hospital. Michael went to Sugars late on a Friday in search of cool air conditioning, a cold drink, and pleasant conversation.

"Are you always so deep in thought?" Michael looked up to see Elaine at his side. "I'm so glad you're here," she said. "Don't move. I'll bring you a margarita on the house. I've got a big favor to ask."

She brought the margarita and sat next to him. "Michael, I need an escort for two other girls and me tonight. It's very important, at the Brazos Hotel. It's a conventioneers fling."

Michael didn't follow. "What do you need me for?"

"A driver and a chaperon."

"You want me to cover your butt if you and your friends get in over your heads. Is that it?"

"Please, Michael. I'll make it worth your while."

Michael thought about the request. Jan would be home early tonight, preparing for a busy weekend. He could always tell Jan he was working late. Elaine touched his arm. He felt her warm breath on his cheek. His brain immediately posted red flags in his field of vision. It wasn't wise to accompany scantily clad females to an unknown rendezvous. He had enough problems without asking for new troubles.

But then, he would be around Elaine. She wouldn't set him up for anything dangerous. There was a maturity about Elaine, all wrapped up in a titillating package. "What time?" Michael asked.

"Pick us up by the side door at midnight."

"That late? That's a little past my bedtime."

"You can do it one night. Please."

"You want me to drive and be your bodyguard while you and your friends entertain some clients for a few hours?"

"Yes, that's all. And bring your gun."

Michael's face tightened. "That's none of your business."

"Okay, okay, but you can carry it into the hotel. I

know you have it on you."

Michael took a long gulp of his drink and whispered into Elaine's ear. "If you're expecting trouble, I'm out."

Elaine shook her head. "I only thought you could pull back your jacket and show it if any of the guys got too rough."

"Does that happen often?"

"No, but just in case."

"I like you Elaine, but you're pushing me to the limit."

Without another word, Elaine kissed him on the cheek. "We'll meet you at the side door. You're special, Michael."

The previous night, Misty had hooked up with three good ole' boys from Big Spring. The men were in Dallas on business and had asked her to come back to their hotel. Misty put them off, got Elaine involved to set up a 'party,' and nailed down the time and place.

Fulfilling parties from arrangements made at the club was a tricky proposition. The idea was to entertain one or two, maybe three married men by playing to their fantasies—costumes, kisses, dances, tits, and lots of skin.

Money, lots of it, was the object. Safety was the catchphrase, which was why the girls always went in groups and took a chauffeur. It wasn't out the question for girls to be drugged, raped, or kidnapped. It had happened before. Having a 'chauffeur' with the group was a wise precaution.

A few minutes past midnight, three women piled into Michael's Acura. Each wore a scarf, dark glasses, and a long, light coat over skimpy costumes. Changes in outfits and wigs were in a large beach bag. Misty lit a smoke. Elaine leaned over and kissed Michael on the cheek. The other girl remained silent.

"You mind not smoking in the car?" Michael said.

"Jeez, I was going to crack the window," Misty replied.

"Girls, this is Michael. Michael, this is Misty who can wait to smoke till we get to the hotel, right? And this is Crystal." At the hotel, Michael parked in an underground garage, and the four of them took the elevator to the top floor.

"They got us the penthouse," Misty beamed. When the elevator door opened, they were met by impressive décor. The hallway carpet was a motif of elegant Persian gold and blue threads. Fragile miniature chandeliers spaced every five feet hung from the ceiling. At Room 1001, Misty stuck the key in the lock.

Grogan and his buddies were waiting. Each of them was seated on one of four love seats arranged in a circle in the center of the room. They were reclined in white Turkish bathrobes, drinking, laughing, and clouding the room with puffs of smoke from enormous cigars.

"Look who's here," said Stevens, a freckled, red-faced man easily pushing forty who raised his drink in greeting.

Grogan turned and rose from his seat. "Evening ladies." His eyes surveyed the three women, and then he saw Michael. "Who's that?"

Misty unbuttoned her coat and revealed a gauzy, red and silver outfit. "He's our driver. I told you about him. Pay him no mind. He'll wait in the anteroom."

Grogan said nothing further. Michael got a glass of water from the kitchenette and sat in a wicker chair in the foyer surrounded by an ivy-covered trellis and ferns.

Stevens stepped to the bar to freshen his drink. "What'cha having?"

"Gin and tonic for me," Elaine said. When he fixed Elaine's drink, he looked to Becky.

"Just club soda," she said.

Misty took a CD from her bag, put it into a CD player next to the TV, and began dancing for Grogan and the third man named Hatch. Stevens beckoned Elaine and Becky into a side bedroom. Six lines of coke were on a mirror. A thin snorting straw and a thimble size bag of white powder lay beside it.

"Here's the deal," Stevens said. "You can do as much of this as you want, but you can't take any with you. We'll pay for the entertainment, but no trying to take advantage of my friends." He looked directly at Elaine.

"Got it," she said. Give us a minute, and we'll join the party."

"I need a pick-me-up first." Stevens snorted one line, then left the room sniffing and clearing his throat.

Elaine took Becky by the shoulders and looked directly into her eyes. "Okay, now. It doesn't get any easier than this. Just put on a show — three guys who will never see you again. No pressure, no sweat. Just do it the way I showed you, nice and slow."

"I will," Becky sucked in a breath. "Who was the guy who brought us?"

"Just a friend of mine," Elaine picked up the straw.

"You said his name is Michael, right?"

"He's just a customer who likes me. There are lots of guys out there like him."

Becky wanted to ask more, but Elaine was consumed with snorting and sniffing. It didn't matter, Becky already knew. She knew the moment she got in the car. The same guy from the house, Lance's hospital bedroom, the one she sat with at the club several days ago. What was he doing here? Why would an IRS federal agent escort a bunch of party girls to a hotel? Maybe she could learn something incriminating about him tonight and reduce her time of employment at the club to a few days of unpleasant memories. He had shot her brother. For that, Becky shared her father's anger. For that, she was willing to get some dirt on him and let her father take it from there.

"You want a hit?" Elaine asked.

"No." Becky shook her head emphatically.

"Put this on." Elaine took a short cut platinum wig from the costume bag. Becky already wore a pair of billowy gold tear-away satin pants and matching long-sleeve shirt with a zipper down the front. Elaine glanced past the bedroom door. "Misty's almost through. Go in there and give'em a show."

Becky swallowed. Her knees were weak. Her skin tingled. Misty changed the music to a slow country ballad, and Becky let her mind disengage from her body as she slipped through the bedroom door to cheers from the men. She moved into the circle formed by the couches, raised her arms in the air, and turned slowly in front of them. Already, she felt naked, but she forced her mind to drift. Although she faced each man in turn, Becky couldn't stand to look any of them in the eye. She bent over and looked through her legs as Elaine had coached. The men took turns sticking bills into her waistband. Shame grew in her belly. She began unzipping her shirt, laboring to move in rhythm with the music.

The men cackled, whistled, and bounced against the overstuffed cushions. Finally unbuttoned, Becky twirled the gold blouse over her head, then sent it flying toward Grogan who yelped with glee and held the garment high above his head like a trophy. After a few more steps, bends and twirls, she ripped off her tear-away pants and flung them toward Stevens, but Grogan sprang from his seat and snatched them from the air.

Becky unsnapped the bow tie she'd been wearing all evening and tossed it to Hatch. Stevens' face fell with animated dejection. Five minutes had passed, yet Becky remained as uncomfortable as the moment she first stepped into the circle.

Now, all she had on were her white boots, red bra, and panties. She didn't want to expose herself to these tongue-wagging, immature morons. She didn't want to take her clothes off in front of anybody. She regretted accepting Elaine's invite to the hotel. For the first time in her life, she despised her father. Why had she agreed to any of this? Again, Becky turned slowly in the circle. Her shoulders felt cold. Her face flushed hot. Pangs of humiliation drummed in her chest as her eyes welled up with wetness. The music pounded in her ears. She reached for the bra snaps between her breasts. The three men yelled approval as she began to pull the bra apart.

The sudden roar of voices scared her and brought her to her senses. She sucked back a sob, turned and jumped across a love seat, and ran from the room. Becky ran past Elaine and into the bedroom where she yanked off a bedspread and covered herself.

Hatch ran after her. Elaine stepped in his way.

"Give her some time. She's new."

"Give her some time, shit. She didn't have no problem taking my money. I want her to finish her dance."

Elaine stood her ground. Hatch towered over her. He was a young buck, mid-twenties with a lanky, wiry build. It was obvious he was headstrong with a one-track mind and probably more than a little stupid. "Tell her to come back out."

"Not right now. Go back and sit down. I'll dance for you."

Hatch pushed Elaine aside and headed for the bedroom. Within two steps, Michael was at his side.

"Wait a minute, Hoss. Give the lady a minute."

Hatch looked at Michael as if he were a bug. "Take a hike, Slim. Goody Two Shoes is going to finish her dance."

"What's the rush, pal? The night's young."

"Butt out, taxi driver. These gals are here to entertain, not run away. I want her to finish what she started."

Grogan and Stevens sat grinning, watching whatever Hatch was going to do. In the bedroom, Becky was terrified. She clutched the bedspread to her throat, unable to see into the living room, but she heard every word.

"Go back and sit down," Michael commanded.

"Like hell, piss ant." Hatch took a swing. He missed with his right, but a roundhouse with his left followed close behind. Hatch's fist caught Michael flush in the neck and knocked him back a step. Michael threw a left that caught Hatch on the chin and buckled his knees.

Elaine flew past them, tossed a coat at Misty, and grabbed her bag. Misty scooped up her clothes and headed for the door. Misty knew as well as Elaine when it was time to abandoned ship.

Hatch was younger, his arms longer, and his punches faster than any counter-attack Michael could mount. But Michael stood against him, deflecting what punches he could, dodging others. Still, Michael's face quickly took a pounding. His nose was bloodied. A welt swelled under his left eye.

"That's enough," cried Misty.

"Shoot him," screamed Elaine.

The words stunned Hatch for an instant. He hesitated. In that split second, Michael threw a right cross that caught Hatch's nose. Elaine sprang for the bar, grabbed a whiskey bottle, and swung it. The bottle caught Hatch in the back of the skull with the power of a bat making perfect contact with an inside fastball. Hatch dropped, unconscious. A puddle of blood began to form in front of his face.

Grogan and Stevens stared at the melee as if dumbstruck. By the time they moved, Michael, and the girls were out of the suite. They'd grabbed their coats and costumes and dashed to the elevator. Elaine got the car keys from Michael's pocket and drove with Misty riding in front. Becky held Michael's head in her lap as she tended his bloody face with a wad of tissues in the backseat of the car. She wore nothing but her underwear and a thin trench coat open in front.

"Does he need to go to the hospital?" Elaine glanced at Becky through the rear view mirror.

"No, no hospital," Michael protested. "I just need an ice pack."

"You can't go home looking like that," Elaine said.

"What are you going to do?" asked Misty.

"Take him to my place, I guess. He needs some ice on that eye real quick."

"Drop me off at the club first, will you?" Misty asked. "I'd help you, but."

"I understand," Elaine replied. "Take in the bag. At least we can get the extra costumes back where they belong."

Misty turned to the backseat. "You did a good job, mister. That jerk's going to have a sore face in the morning."

"So am I."

"Yeah, but you made him pay for being such a

creep. You did good with that bottle, Elaine."

"Lucky shot," Elaine laughed.

Becky found no levity in the situation. It was difficult to make sense of what had happened. Here she was, holding the battered head of a man she barely knew — a man who stood up for her when he didn't have to. Even more disconcerting, she could find no appreciation in her heart for his selfless act. Deep inside, she felt pleased that he'd been beaten. Michael lay with his head in her lap, groaning softly, but not complaining, not blaming anyone.

When they got to the club, Misty got out. Elaine turned to the backseat. "Is your car here or do you need me to take you somewhere?"

"Oh," Becky said. "I don't want to duck out and leave you with him to handle. I'll go with you."

CHAPTER TWENTY-TWO

$

ELAINE LIVED IN A ROW OF OLDER TOWNHOUSES surrounded by drooping, broken down elms not far from Love Field. Elaine opened the door while Becky helped Michael inside. His nose quit bleeding, but the welt under his eye swelled to the size of a potato wedge. His lip was cut, and he held his jaw with his hand.

Elaine led him to the bedroom and helped him lie down and stretch out. She grabbed a makeup encrusted pillow and tucked it under his head. Becky quickly dressed in a pair of green satin shorts from Elaine's dresser, threw off the coat, and zipped up a windbreaker. The women met in the kitchen and made ice packs with plastic bags wrapped in towels and adjusted them around Michael's face.

"Why didn't you shoot him?" Elaine asked once

they had tended his cuts and iced his face.

The mention of a gun immediately unnerved Becky. Michael uttered a muffled groan.

"Let me look at you again," Elaine lifted each ice bag and studied his wounds. Every inch of his face had taken a beating. Dried blood caked his chin. His face remained pinched in pain, but his breathing was steady. "That was assault, Michael. He had no right to charge after Crystal, and no right to hit you. If you'd cocked that piece, he'd have changed his tune."

"You've been watching too much TV," Michael murmured.

"Have I? That son-of-a-bitch oughta go to jail."

"Please, let me rest."

"Michael, why didn't you pull your gun? You had every right, and it probably would have saved you such a beating."

"It's for official business only. I didn't bring it anyway. I wouldn't have brought it even if I knew there was going to be trouble."

"Didn't bring it? I don't know if you're brave or stupid."

"Leave me alone," he said. "The gun is none of your business."

Elaine said nothing more, but stood over Michael, hands on hips, shaking her head.

Becky didn't know what to make of it either. She knew he had been trigger happy and careless before. Tonight, however, he took a whipping for three women he barely knew rather than use everything at his disposal to defend himself. The two women looked at each other, then again at Michael. His blood soaked shirt disappeared under a mound of ice bags across his upper chest. Becky took off his shoes and placed them in the corner.

"Well, I need a smoke and a shower," Elaine said. "Will you watch him for a while?"

Becky nodded as she knelt beside the bed. She brushed a tangle of sweaty hair back from his eyes and ran her fingers across his forehead. It was him alright; as she had known. He had angular features on a tanned face. He was neither handsome nor average. There was something noble about his chin and cheekbones. His pathetic appearance brought a brief pang of caring in her breast, and Becky ran her fingers across his forehead again. Her thoughts of his previous careless actions softened as she gazed upon his battered, defeated form. His eye looked ghastly. The contusion under the eye was full of blood. It would have to be cut open or drained with a needle. As minutes passed, it was increasingly impossible for her to maintain the chill in her heart after what he had done for her this night. Still, she hadn't reached the altar of forgiveness. She also knew her father would have no sympathy what-so-ever for his condition.

When Elaine asked Becky to go with her and Misty to a hotel party, she agreed without thinking. It provided an opportunity to get out of the club, less time to be at home — fewer encounters with her father's accusations and irrational rants.

She studied Michael's battered face as she continued to stroke his forehead and realized she was lying to herself. She was feeling. She did care. A tingle of tenderness welled up inside her as tears came to her eyes. Why in the hell was this man even at the hotel? Why did he have to be her knight in shining armor? Why couldn't he have let her be forced to humiliate herself? Becky ran to the kitchen. She turned both faucets on full blast and let the mascara and rouge swirl down the drain mixed with tears. After she dried her face, she heard him groan over the sound of Elaine's running shower.

"Can I get you something," she said.

"Some Tylenol or something sure would help."

Becky passed Elaine in the hall, went to the bathroom, and attacked the medicine cabinet. Three tiny glass shelves behind the mirror were stuffed with outdated prescriptions, unused cotton swabs, messy lipstick tubes, and several nasal sprays. She counted two squeezed-out, rolled-up toothpaste tubes. Didn't Elaine ever use a wastebasket? Behind throat lozenges, Becky found generic aspirin and Tylenol. She would give Michael a couple of Tylenol.

When Becky returned to the bedroom, Elaine was in bed beside Michael, under the covers and curled up beside him.

"Is he cold?"

"No, but I am."

Becky rolled her eyes. "Take these." Becky knelt and helped Michael sit up enough to swallow the pills. "I'm going to lie down on the couch for now."

"I'll keep him warm," Elaine said.

Becky didn't respond. It occurred to her she wanted the two of them together in bed. Maybe she was about to free herself from a nightmare, and compromising photographs might do it. She had her smartphone in her bag. She would photograph his beat-up face and show him in bed with another woman. Her father would be elated. He could work his hateful schemes, and she would be out of it. As long as she escaped the degrading work where she now found herself, she would take the pictures. She would implicate this man in transgressions not of his making and hope it was enough.

Fifteen minutes later, Becky checked the bedroom. Both Michael and Elaine seemed fast asleep. Becky knelt beside Michael's knees and took several pictures of his face. Then she stood above them and took shots of their heads together. Finally, Becky took pictures from the foot of the bed.

She watched as Michael slowly raised an arm and motioned her to come his way. Becky hid the camera behind her back.

"Help me up."

She slipped to his side and pushed more pillows behind his back.

"That's enough," he said as he kept one ice bag on his eye and let two others under his jaw fall across his chest and onto the bed.

"Could I get another glass of water?"

Becky brought back the largest glass she could find, and he drained it in one long gulp. Michael looked straight into her eyes. "I wanted to know who it was I took this whipping for."

Becky almost laughed at his quip and would have, but he looked so pathetic, so damaged. His eye would be black and blue for the better part of a month. His lip may need stitches. "I'm Crystal. I'm so sorry you got hurt on my account." Without a second thought, the words fell from her lips with complete sincerity. She had no intention of telling him who she was, but she also felt no joy over the beating he had endured. This gentle-spoken man defended her against a potential rapist. Becky no longer saw the careless thug who came to her house that morning.

Elaine's body jerked beside him as she pulled the covers to her face. She quickly settled back down. Elaine was crashing heavy, taking up two-thirds of the bed.

"Have I met you at the club?" Michael asked.

"Let's not talk now. Lay back down." Becky knelt behind him and helped him fully recline. She placed an ice bag over his lip and cheek and another under his jaw. Michael raised his hand and touched her arm and slid his hand into hers.

"Your hand's so cold," he said.

His hand was soft yet strong. She didn't reply.

Becky placed the last of the ice bags over his eye held in place by a pillow. "Now get some rest and let the ice work. I'm going to lie down in front."

Becky took one last look at him before she turned out the table lamp. She slipped into the kitchen and called a taxi. All the time she waited at the window, she wondered if by chance he had caught her taking pictures. When the taxi arrived, Becky quietly let herself out into the cool breaking dawn of a new day.

****

Becky arrived home just before six. Now she was nervous for another reason. If her father caught her in the short satin pants and calf-high white boots, coming in at this hour, he'd either fly into a rage or give her the condescending, silent treatment. She snuck through the side gate, in the back door nearer the stairs with less of the house to walk through. She was almost to the bottom step when Cleet cleared his throat and turned on a table lamp.

"I thought you got off at eleven?" he said.

Becky jumped and fell against the staircase. "We had a late party. I had to go."

"What kind of party?" As Becky stood and turned, a shaft of morning light came through the blinds and fell upon her. "My god, you're a sight."

"It's only part of a costume. You didn't need to wait down here all night."

"It looks like I did." His voice rose in volume. "You're not responsible at all, are you?"

"Stop it. I'm doing what you wanted, so leave me alone." An awkward silence filled the room. Finally, she said, "I got some photographs of that IRS agent."

"Really?"

"He was there tonight. He got into a fight and beat up pretty bad."

"That's great," Cleet said as his expression turned to delighted anticipation.

Becky shook her head in disgust. "You're unbearable. You look at them. I'm going to bed." Becky grabbed the smartphone from her bag and tossed it to her father.

"That's great," Cleet repeated. He fondled the phone as though it were a special present. Becky and her whereabouts last night completely left his mind. Cleet sat in the chair beside the table lamp. His eyes lit up, and a smile came to his lips as he flipped through the pictures on the phone.

CHAPTER TWENTY-THREE

$

AS MORNING LIGHT POKED THROUGH THE CURTAINS, Michael's face throbbed with every beat of his heart. He couldn't move. His shoulders ached. His mind struggled to connect his body to his surroundings. The instant he touched his jaw the memories of the previous night flew at him.

With eyes closed, he reached for the warm, damp bag on his neck and placed it on the floor. A hangover would not have been any more nauseating and a lot less painful. He forced himself to sit, then stand, and made his way to the bathroom.

The sight of his face in the mirror made him wince. A twinge of fear darted up his spine. He had taken a beating and returned maybe one good punch. He needed to see a doctor. Blood had collected in a pocket under the skin below his eye. He touched lightly around the edges of his injuries. What had Elaine said about escorting girls to the hotel? A bunch of nice guys, nothing to it, lots of fun. How was he going to explain this? What was he going to say to Jan?

His stomach grumbled, so he made his way to the kitchen and opened the refrigerator. There was plenty of Coors Light, club soda, and ready-made margarita mix. He found ketchup, mustard, an empty jar of salad dressing, tartar sauce, steak sauce, chocolate syrup, and pickle relish, and not a damn thing to eat. When he turned around, Elaine was there, pulling a bathrobe around her naked body. Modesty was a word that had left her vocabulary long ago.

"Oh, Michael, you poor baby." She sounded truly concerned. "I'll make you breakfast."

Elaine located bagels and pop tarts in the pantry and dropped them in the toaster. She made him breakfast out of beer and bread. Michael called downtown and told Barnes' secretary he was sick. He called Jan and told her he was downtown. She sounded busy and indifferent and didn't ask where he'd been all night. Michael called his doctor and made an emergency appointment.

"A pretty nice place, don't you think?" Elaine said over nibbles on her bagel.

"Sure, it's nice." Michael hadn't noticed and didn't care. "Don't you have anything else to eat?"

"Some potato chips."

"No, thanks." He kept chewing on a bland pop tart.

"Michael," she said. "I know you come to see me because you like me best of all the girls at the club. I want you to know I really like you, too."

"Thanks." He couldn't think of anything else to say. He looked closer at Elaine across the dinette table. The morning light gave her face a harder edge, more blotchy than one would notice at the club. She was still young with sparkling blue eyes, dimpled cheeks, and a cute nose. But the daily drinking and late hours were making inroads on her complexion. She was giving away her youth to hordes of anonymous men who had no interest in her as a person.

"You're always so nice and polite to me," she continued. "I thought that maybe sometime we could go out regular like."

What? Why was she starting this? His face looked like freshly ground hamburger, yet she wanted to make some personal confessions and ask him for a date. He could say he was married, but she knew that. From that standpoint, the relationship they already had was bad enough.

"Not now, Elaine. I feel terrible. I need to get to my doctor."

"I'm so sorry this happened. It's all my fault." She moved around the table and kissed him on the cheek. "Let me get dressed, and I'll take you there. You're in no condition to drive."

****

Frank Masters sat in his second floor apartment surrounded by old newspapers and cigar butts. He and Michael were getting behind in tax dollars collected, and cases closed. Frank flipped through a spiral-bound notebook and made mental notes on outstanding cases. Michael's shooting escapade hadn't helped in resolving their workload. Every day since it happened, Frank found himself rehashing events for different groups of investigators that crawled from every black hole in the federal government.

Barnes' accusatory, complaining attitude grated on Frank's nerves. It was as if it was Frank's fault Michael had gotten nervous, lost his cool, and fired his handgun in a private residence. Frank never cared for Barnes anyway, primarily because Barnes had never been a Revenue Officer or Special Agent. Barnes' first six years with the IRS had been spent as an auditor. He had the good fortune of making the personal acquaintance of Benson Montgomery. At the time, Montgomery was the Director of the entire Midwest Region. Through the game of bridge, of all things, their wives had become good friends. As far as Frank was concerned, Barnes had lip locked the old man's ass for eighteen months and road it upstairs to the Dallas District Supervisor position.

Any reasonably competent bureaucrat with a demonstrated proclivity for paper shuffling would qualify for Barnes' position. Though Frank hated the thought of being assigned to a desk, he knew he understood better than Barnes what it took to get their job done. It was in that knowledge he found a measure of comfort to repress the disgust he felt for Barnes.

Added to everything else, Bill Raney called night and day as though Frank was the accountant's personal gopher. The very fact Raney needed him so often made it clear that Raney's tax-avoidance schemes were out of control. All Frank wanted out of Raney was some extra dough. If Raney was in danger of going down, Frank had no intention of sinking with him.

Frank was well aware of where he fell in the grand scheme of things. He was a revenue mercenary employed by the feds to do their dirty work under a veil of legal mumbo-jumbo. Let Michael dizzy himself with tortured mental gymnastics as he tried to make sense of the tax system. Frank knew better. There was no common sense or equality in the system. Some people paid; some people didn't. Some paid more; some paid less. The rules were complex, confusing, and arbitrarily applied. To think everyone at the same income level paid the same tax was a sure sign of encroaching dementia.

Frank realized the only way to relieve his stress was to get back to work. He circled some names on his list and prioritized them for the day. He was through talking to them. Today, he would shut them down if they didn't write him a check for the full amount owed the federal treasury. He grabbed his revolver from the desk drawer, checked the chamber, and jammed it into his shoulder holster. He checked the coffee pot to make sure it was off and left the apartment. Today would not be a good day for a delinquent taxpayer to play games with Frank Masters.

First stop was Bill Raney's office. Frank wanted to set the tone for the day, and he would do just that with Raney.

Frank thought about the many times he'd made unannounced appearances and put the fear of god into the taxpayers Raney called clients. More times than he cared to remember. On every unofficial visit, he risked being exposed, reported on, fired, brought up on charges of illegal and unauthorized use of his official position, and ultimately thrown in jail.

Frank was well aware of the risk he took, which was why he always overplayed the intimidation. He browbeat people to such a point, upon his departure, they were thankful not to be led away in cuffs. Once he flashed his badge and said the magic words 'IRS' every citizen who played in the gray areas of the tax code became as meek and obedient as little girls in Sunday school.

But Frank knew he'd been lucky, too. One call downtown and his backdoor game of pressure and extortion could quickly fall apart. His profitable relationship with Raney was becoming too risky. Raney was under increasing pressure from his clients. Raney said so himself. If his clients were unhappy or grasping for a fall guy, any one of them could generate an investigation into Raney's entire practice. It was time to cut the cord. He would deal with Raney this morning the same way he dealt with deadbeat taxpayers every day for the past twenty-eight years.

As he drove up, Frank spotted Raney's Buick SUV in the parking lot. The office door was locked.

Frank rapped a syncopated knock and saw the vertical blind move at the far end of the window glass. Raney let him in, glanced both ways down the street, and quickly closed the door.

"Good morning, my friend," Raney said without enthusiasm. He led the way to the back office. "Did you have any problems?" Raney moved behind his desk while Frank stood behind a chair.

Frank ignored the question. "We have to talk."

"What now?" Raney's words oozed defeat.

"I'm not your personal errand boy for one thing. I don't have time for all your crap. Why are you getting so much guff from your clients all of a sudden?"

"Well, it's not all of a sudden, really. It's been building. I didn't think so many of them would get audited in the same year."

"What do you mean 'so many of them'?"

"I don't know. A few." Raney dropped his head.

"How many?" Frank demanded.

"Fifty, I think."

"How in the hell many clients do you have?"

Raney swallowed, then said. "A hundred and sixty."

Frank stepped to the front of Raney's desk. "What have you been doing?" Frank screamed. A distinct sensation of fear rolled through his gut. Almost a third of Raney's clients had been red-flagged by the Service. Raney's whole operation was about to blow. There was no way to contain it. If a third of his customers got hit with deficiency judgments, someone would surely talk. Everyone would be looking for a scapegoat. In-depth investigations would follow.

Frank placed his hands on the desk, ready to pulverize the first thing he could get his strong, stubby fingers around. "What kind of games have you been playing all these years?" Frank swiped at a stapler and sent it crashing against the wall.

"It's the same stuff other accountants have been doing," Raney stammered. "The rules got changed, tax opinions from the IRS were different from what we expected, deductions were disallowed."

"I don't believe you. You've been playing fast and loose with the rules, and now you've got your nuts in a vice, and you want me to save your pathetic hide."

"You've got it all wrong. I'm just doing my job, aggressively, I admit, but just trying to save my customers money. That's what I'm supposed to do."

"I'm out. I'm out, and you're going to forget you ever knew me." Frank drew back his jacket, exposing the butt or his gun, and old man Raney all but fainted in his chair.

"You—you want more money?" Raney said.

"I said I'm out. With the fix you've gotten yourself into, I say you're going down. But you're not taking me with you. I helped you string people along, but the problems you got are all your own doing."

"Don't cut out on me now," Raney whined. "I got this one guy who's stirring up extra trouble. He acts like I owe him special favors, like I caused all his problems, which ain't true. He's the biggest problem I got. You could make him shut up. I'll pay you $5,000 to make him crawl back in his hole and leave me alone. Here, listen to this."

Raney reached under the desk, flipped a switch, and a tape recording began to play. Frank's eyes widened as he listened to a conversation between Raney and another man about a boy in the hospital. As the recording went along, the volume of the voices increased, and the other man told Raney his best course of action was to skim money from his other clients to get the man's tax deficiency paid.

"Where'd you get that," Frank demanded.

"I made it right here. The guy was in here three days ago,"

"He's your client?"

"Yeah— well, he was."

"You're making recordings of conversations in your office?" The question was rhetorical. Frank's thoughts tumbled. He struggled to refocus after receiving the biggest shock of his clandestine and illegal career.

"Have to protect myself, that's all. The tapes are safe. Nobody's going to hear them unless I want them to be heard," Raney said.

Frank could feel the heat building under his collar. Raney was as stupid as he was crooked. Anyone of a half dozen governmental agencies with jurisdiction and an interest in his business could get a court order. They could raid his office and seize every document, file, and computer disk in the place. Those recordings were a ticking time bomb. If Frank's voice were on any of them, it would guarantee him a one-way ticket to prison.

"So he's putting the screws to you about putting up the money he owes?" Frank asked.

"Yeah, and I know he intends to hurt me if I don't, but there's no way I can come up with eighty grand out of thin air in the time he's given me."

"And that is?"

"Thirty days. I just—I just want him out of my hair for good. I can take care of all the rest." A long pause hung between the two men, then Raney continued. "I know he got a visit from your office and his boy got hurt, but if he'd dealt with you people from the beginning, none of that would have happened. Right?"

Frank nodded. He had regained control of his emotions and thoughts. Now he had a plan.

"Who shot the boy? Was it you?" Raney asked.

"No, it wasn't me, and I wouldn't tell you anyway."

"All right, but the five grand. Make him go away—permanently. I think he's unstable. One last job, okay? One last job."

Frank hesitated. He had to make sure he did this right. "All right, one last job. But I want the money up front."

Raney swallowed. "You'll do it?"

"Yeah, I'll run him off."

"I don't want him just run off. I want him permanently out of commission. I never want to see him in the office again."

"When I say I'll take care of it, I'll take care of it. You'll never see or hear from him again."

Raney sat back in his chair. His whole body seemed to relax. Some color appeared in his sallow cheeks. "Great, but I don't have that much cash here."

"So, when? When can you get it?"

"By tonight. Come back just after seven. I'll have it all then."

"So what's this guy's name," Frank asked, knowing full well who it was. Frank glared at Raney and ran his tongue hard across his teeth like he was licking peanut butter off his gums.

"Cletus Dixon. He runs a metal fabrication shop near North Stemmons and Walnut Hill."

"Okay, I'll be back after seven. Get the money and I'll take care of this guy. Then I don't want to ever hear from you again. And you better get those other cases resolved." With that, Frank let himself out the back.

Frank sat in his car and lit a cigar while his heart rate diminished and he tried to figure his next move. Dixon may truly pose the biggest threat and the first person most likely to bring down Raney's house of cards. Already Dixon was talking to every reporter or cop who would listen.

It was just one small step for him to complain about Raney's business practices and for a formal investigation to commence. A man who's son has been shot by a federal agent can attract many attentive ears. At that moment, Frank knew he had to keep tabs on Dixon's every move until he found the right opportunity to act.

CHAPTER TWENTY-FOUR

$

IF CLEET HAD BEEN THE LEAST BIT SLEEPY, the photographs changed all that. He washed his face, dressed in a burnt-orange Texas Longhorn shirt and gray slacks, and hurried into the morning light to the incessant chirping of birds. Any beauty in the early hour escaped him.

He drove to a drug store and talked to an attendant at the photo kiosk. She would make photo enlargements of all the pictures in the camera and have them ready by noon. Cleet drove to his office. He intended to handle any important paperwork on his desk, but all he could think about was the photographs being enlarged and printed. When he heard voices in the hall, he glanced at the clock. It was a few minutes before eight. He slipped out a side door and went back to his car.

At a nearby diner, Cleet ate breakfast and read the Morning News from front to back. When he arrived back at the drug store, the pictures were ready. He flipped through the snapshots and let out a raucous laugh. The sight of Cranfield's swollen eye and cut lip filled his heart with joy. It was his happiest moment in the past ten days. He had two envelopes already stamped and addressed. He dropped several photos into each one and took them straight to the post office.

Now—one more thing.

****

When Becky awoke, it was past noon. If the pictures she gave to her father made him happy, it would be a miracle. Nothing made him happy anymore. If the pictures accomplished what he wanted—then fine. She was beyond caring one way or the other. She fully intended to move on, escape his demands. She was making money, and she could make more. No longer would she remain tied to her father's financial support.

She couldn't help thinking about Michael. He seemed like such an oddball, and yet so gallant. She was thankful he was at the hotel and willing to defend her, a stripper he didn't know, in a situation, she was sure, he hadn't fully bargained for. It didn't change her opinion of his reckless act that injured Lance, but now she saw him differently. She had the day off from the club and would spend most of her time with Lance at the hospital. But she wanted to see this strange hero again. She wanted to know that he too was all right.

Becky was sure he would realize in short order who took the pictures, photographs that would undoubtedly show up in embarrassing and unexpected places. She didn't want to hear about that, especially after what he had done for her. She had no honorable explanations for her actions. Now, she was emotionally torn. It might be best to avoid him entirely, dismiss the thought of him completely. And yet, he was the only person to unselfishly come to her aid after days of rejection and sadness.

****

Cleet drove to a pawn shop he passed every day. Stuck behind another driver at a four-way stop, Cleet laid into the horn until the car finally moved. He sped past and flipped off the driver. At the last moment, Cleet saw it was an old woman, eyes wide in terror, both hands gripping the wheel. As he neared the pawn shop, he darted across two lanes of traffic without signaling.

If this place had a handgun fairly large in caliber and small in profile, he'd take it. Cleet knew there would be a background check and waiting period. Better to buy it now so he'd have the gun when the time was right.

Even if a pawn shop was in an attractive building, as far as Cleet was concerned, they were all junk barns inside. Hand tools dumped haphazardly into crates along one wall, obsolete computers on the other. There were small-headed, worn-out golf clubs that no one who knew the game would be caught dead using, power tools with frayed cords, grimy microwaves, overpriced guitars, and mounds of videotapes stacked upside down so you couldn't read the titles.

An exception to the dusty assortment of pawned junk was the jewelry and gun cases. After all, jewelry and guns were the store's high margin items.

The gun case was lined with black velvet. Embossed brown and black holsters lay beside the firearms. Military style weapons were on one side of the case, Western revolvers on the other. The impressive display encouraged a person to buy a gun even if a person had never considered it before.

"How much for that one?" Cleet asked.

"Three eighty, sir."

"How many rounds does it hold?"

"Five." The clerk took the gun from the case.

It was beautiful. A silver .38 slightly larger than Cleet's hand. The weight felt perfect.

"I'll take it." Cleet handed the clerk a card from his wallet.

The clerk swiped the card, typed on the keypad, and began to frown. "Sorry, sir. It didn't authorize. Says the account's closed."

"What the hell. Try this one."

The clerk repeated the procedure with the same result. "Is this card through the same bank?"

"Yes," Cleet replied.

"Says it's closed too."

"Them sons a bitches," Cleet said under his breath. He flipped through the cash in his wallet. "What'cha got for under two hundred?"

"Just this twenty-two. It's one-forty plus tax."

The gun had a six inch barrel and a dull gray finish that looked like plastic. "That's all you have for two hundred?"

"That's all, sir."

Cleet didn't say another word. He paid for the gun and filled out the paperwork. All the while large drops of sweat beaded up on his forehead and he face got redder by the minute.

Thirty minutes later, Cleet was at the hospital. He pushed the door open quietly in case Lance was resting, but found him watching baseball on TV.

"Hey, how are you doing?"

"Feeling a lot better, really. The nurse got me out of bed earlier. Walked down the hall with a walker and her by my side. Sure was nice to get out of bed."

"Well good. How did it feel?"

"Stiff and sore, but it didn't hurt much."

"That's good to hear," Cleet's voice faded as he recalled what the doctor told him yesterday. The bullet had cracked Lance's hip bone near the femur socket. Lance would walk again, likely with a limp. Running would be difficult and should be discouraged. The hip would never be as strong as before, and too much stress might cause it to fracture.

Strands of hair fell into Lance's eyes as the whining purr of the bed motor raised his head higher. He rolled slightly off his injured hip. "I'll be good as new in time," Lance said. "I start regular physical therapy sessions this afternoon."

"Good. Just do what the doctor says. Don't try to overdo anything and have another relapse."

Lance considered the advice. "Yeah, but I'm starting to get really bored around here."

"The nurses are doing their job," Cleet said. "You'll be out of here soon enough'

Lance grimaced and adjusted himself in bed. "Dad?"

"Yes."

"Am I going to be all right?"

"Of course. You're over the worst. Every day you'll be getting back to your old self."

"I know my hip splintered and they removed bone fragments. That's not good, but it will all heal up, right?"

"You were shot, Lance. Some people might think you're lucky to be alive."

"But I feel fine. The pain in my leg is going away. I just want to know what's going on."

"Shot by a tax collector in our own house—"

Instantly, Lance realized his father had left their conversation and was talking to himself. Lance could do nothing but watch his dad sway in place with tense, tortured movements. Cleet's hands were clenched on the metal foot rail, his head raised, having a solitary conversation with the light bulb in the ceiling.

"—I support my community. I employ a lot of hard working people." Cleet's head dropped and he stared at his shoes. "We've been paying on this supposed tax debt—in my own home— from an employee of my government—in my own home."

"Dad, I'm okay. Listen to me. I'm getting

better."

Cleet's eyes flashed open and a stark sadness fell over his face so pitiful and profound. Lance had seen it but once before—at his mother's funeral.

"The doctor says you'll probably never run again."

An awkward silence punctuated the end of his sentence, but the doctor's pessimistic prognosis was of less concern to Lance than it was to his father. "When I can walk on my own, we'll see."

"Didn't you hear what I said, boy? That SOB crippled you. For what? For money I don't owe. Damn Gestapo tactics, that son-of-a-bitch."

"I'm not a cripple," Lance yelled in an attempt to shake his father from his gloomy diatribe.

"Dear god, I hope not, but the doctor says you'll have to give up sports."

"I can deal with it."

"Lance, you're not listening. You're in here for no good reason, no good reason at all."

"Take it easy, dad. I'll get through this, you'll see."

Cleet shook a clinched fist. "Great, but what the hell is good about getting shot? Do you have any idea what this has done to me? And the way. . ." Cleet stopped abruptly and rubbed his face with both hands. After a long pause, he spoke again. "I'm going to go now. I hope I haven't upset you too much, son, but I know I probably have. Get your rest and don't worry about me. I'll be all right, and I'll be back tomorrow."

"Dad, I'm going to be okay." Already his father was gone, and Lance's words drifted into an empty hallway as the huge oak door swung closed.

CHAPTER TWENTY-FIVE

$

THE INTERNAL REVENUE SERVICE was always behind. The constant struggle within all offices was not to lag even further. The exponential growth of the tax paying public grew unabated. Revisions, interpretations, and tax code rulings changed constantly, festered like an open wound, the scab scraped back every few months, never allowed to fully heal. If taxpayers lived in a state of confusion, the employees of the Service fared no better. IRS employees lived in an environment of structured chaos, like playing a football game where the rules changed every quarter.

Barnes reviewed the file in front of him. It was the last official matter Michael Cranfield had closed. Barnes hadn't seen Michael since he was dispatched to seize Dixon's bank account. He wanted to know Michael was earning his keep and "feeding the beast" of the U.S. Federal Treasury. But there was another reason, too. Barnes grabbed his desk phone and dialed Michael's home number.

Michael's face felt like he'd been pummeled with a sand-filled sock. He forced himself to sit, put his feet on the floor, and found he wasn't in his own bed, but on the couch in the den. Surely, Jan had seen him there. She hadn't cared enough to inquire about his bruises. In a way, he'd have rather been awakened and scolded than to again be ignored.

He went to the bedroom and stood in front of a full-length wall mirror. The sight of his black eye made him recoil in shock. The doctor had drained the pocket of blood from under his eye with a syringe, but the procedure hardly improved his appearance. Michael ran his finger along his puffy lip. It felt tender, yet normal, compared to the ache in his jaw.

He spent yesterday with Elaine going to the doctor's office, the pharmacy, then back to her house. Elaine really was a sweet soul. For the entire day she was there for him. She kissed his cheeks more times than he could count. Michael saw her for more than the stripper she had become. With Elaine, he had a platonic friendship where he could receive sympathetic words and bare his soul in candid conversation. He held her as they watched afternoon TV before they both fell off to sleep. Later, Elaine dressed for work and they drove to

Sugars. Michael gave her a long embrace as they stood by her car. But that was all he could do, though he saw in Elaine's eyes the longing for a kiss or affectionate parting words. He valued his marriage and still wanted to save it. Michael released her and walked to his car.

Michael returned home after dark. Anything to avoid Jan and the girls seeing his battered face. Now, after a restless night of sleep on the couch, Michael rubbed his temples then set about to find some pain relievers. In the hall bathroom he found only children's aspirin. Children's aspirin wasn't going to do the job. The doctor had prescribed Lortabs, but only six, which he had already taken. In the master bathroom he found a bottle of 500 mg Tylenol and quickly popped two in his mouth.

The phone rang, and he rushed to answer it, fully expecting Jan's voice at the other end of the line.

"Morning, Cranfield. Glad I caught you."

The voice was unmistakable. It was Barnes. Michael glanced at the clock. It was almost eight. Barnes was no doubt calling from his office, there bright and early even on a Saturday.

"I need to catch up on a few things. One of them includes speaking with you before Monday morning."

Michael couldn't utter a response and held the receiver away from his ear like a smelly rag. Not today; not now. He didn't want to talk to anyone, certainly not Barnes.

"I want you to come in this morning so we can have a private chat—just you and me."

"I'm here with my girls and they're still

sleeping."

"Cranfield, we have to talk—today. I'll be here till noon. Make some arrangements and get here as soon as you can. Am I clear?"

The line went dead. A flood of conflicting thoughts pressed inside his aching head. A meeting—in the office—on a Saturday morning. Michael figured he was going to be fired, but what if officers were there from Internal Investigations ready to arrest him? He started to call Barnes back, then changed his mind. Michael darted to the bathroom, bent over the commode with both hands on the seat, and threw up.

When he returned to the den, he called Jan's cell phone. She answered after the sixth ring.

"Is the house on fire?"

What a curt way to answer the phone, he thought. Jan certainly didn't talk that way to clients. But Michael didn't want to argue or listen to another rant.

"I have to go downtown as soon as possible. When can you be here?"

After a long pause, she said, "I'll be there in twenty minutes."

Michael showered, dressed, and found a pair of sunglasses in a bottom dresser drawer. It was the best he could do to hide his facial injuries.

Michael prayed Barnes would be alone. If he were fired, he would manage somehow. But the thought of being taken to jail had his heart pounding under his ribs. The elevator door opened upon a bay of dimly lit office cubicles. Michael felt the clammy wetness of perspiration running down his sides.

Barnes was elbow-deep in paperwork when Michael came in. Barnes didn't quit scribbling until Michael was standing in front of his desk.

"Have a seat." Barnes pushed a stack of folders to one side and extended his hairy arms across the desk. He didn't preface his comments with small talk. He didn't empathize or criticize. The way Barnes had it figured, the sooner he spouted bad tidings, the sooner the monkey was off of his back.

"Cranfield, I got to let you go."

The words hit Michael with a nauseating dump of bile in his guts. He tried to speak. His sore lips moved but were void of sound.

"The internal report came back," Barnes continued. "No criminal complaint, but the finding states your actions were careless and needlessly endangered the public. I've got to have your badge and gun."

"He threatened me," Michael protested. "Does the report reflect that?"

Barnes stoic expression didn't change. "I don't make the findings, but I do have to follow orders."

He could appeal the decision but he knew the outcome was unlikely to change. "That's it?"

Barnes dropped his gaze for a moment. "I can put you in the data entry group if you want to maintain your benefits, but I got to take you off the street."

Data entry group, it would mean a cut in pay. The arrangement would be so awkward that Michael was mortified by the very idea. It would be like telling a dismissed school principal he could stick around if he didn't mind becoming the janitor.

"What happened to your face?" Barnes asked as though the question had just occurred to him.

"Got in a fight."

"That much I figured. How'd it happen?"

Michael shook his head, reluctant to rehash the details.

"Maybe this is the time you reassess your priorities in life, Cranfield. You've got a family. Stay home with them. Don't be doing whatever is getting you in the deep end. As for the Service, we have to have stable, reliable people. We can't have agents with quick tempers or hair triggers."

Michael glared, but knew a verbal defense was useless. Barnes was running his mouth on autopilot, offering up trite phrases to make himself feel better about the whole situation.

"Even if this Dixon incident hadn't happened, I think you need a break," Barnes continued. "Maybe another line of work would better suit you. Not everyone is cut out for this job over the long haul."

Michael took a deep breath. "Can I think about the other assignment over the weekend?"

"Sure. If you're here Monday morning, I'll introduce you to Horton. If not, I'll start processing your severance paperwork."

CHAPTER TWENTY-SIX

$

MICHAEL STUCK HIS KEYS in his car's ignition and sat there. What would he do now? Apply to be a police officer? Maybe a security guard? Oh yeah, the money was great in that line of work. He could see himself as a floor salesman at Home Depot showing carpet samples to housewives or demonstrating dishwashers.

He looked at the folder on the seat beside him, the folder with the names of businesses he and Frank had shut down and padlocked in the past month. He may not be able to help the Dixons directly, but he could bring relief to a few hard working small businesses that had been crushed under the boot of the federal government. Michael started his car. He didn't need to look up addresses.

When he saw the name on the sheet, he knew exactly where the business was. He headed off to remove some padlocks and tear down some signs.

As he drove Michael increasingly felt a fool, what a dupe. Why did he get himself into such a line of work? Collecting tax revenue was never about what the government needed to operate. It's all about what they can get. Even with the hundreds of billions of dollars collected every year, the blood-sucking politicians can't live within their means. They consistently raid funds set aside for other purposes and years ago they figured out how they could sell bonds and borrow more money, in essence, mortgaging the country's future. And for what? To build superfluous projects and name them after well-connected politicians, grant lucrative contracts to high-class donors, and study the sex life of grasshoppers.

Michael's first stop was Beasley's Cabinet Shop. Michael had the keys and he removed the locks from the front and back doors and removed the DO NOT ENTER signs. He felt alive as he made the rounds. The endeavor was more therapeutic than a hot bath and a cold margarita. Later, he would anonymously telephone every business owner and let them know that their taxes were still due, but their places of business were open so they could go back to work.

It was late afternoon when he returned home. Michael took two Tylenol, dropped into bed with his shoes on, and quickly fell asleep.

The sound of a car pulling into the garage awoke him. Michael lay motionless, and stared blankly at the ceiling. Clear across the house, he could hear a bustle of activity when the kitchen door opened. A surge of voices accompanied rapid footsteps that proceeded up the hallway, then the bedroom door flew open.

"There you are," Jan said as though she'd found a naughty puppy hiding under a bed. All the commotion died away as Jan stood in the doorway and the girls scurried to their room.

Michael could hardly see out of his good eye. He didn't look her way. He closed his eyes and ignored her comment. "I'm trying to get some rest."

Jan approached the bed and threw the contents of an envelope at him. "Just what the hell do you call this?" Papers rained upon him.

Michael sat up holding his head in one hand. Then he saw the photographs of his battered face taken within hours of the fistfight. The blood blister under his eye was huge compared to what Jan saw now, but it was the details in the photos that had her blood at a boil. Michael winced when he saw Elaine in the bed, under the covers beside him.

"You're playing around, aren't you?"

"No." Michael got to his feet.

"We're leaving. I'm taking the girls. I'm not living with someone who risks everything I've worked for and lies about what he's been doing."

"What? Jan, it's not what you think."

She wasn't listening, just talking."Working late? Isn't that what you said? How about getting into fights? Getting your damn picture taken in bed with some strange woman? She looks like you picked her up off the street." Jan's face flamed beet red as her features contorted with rage. "You're a loose cannon and a liar. You can't be trusted."

"You can't just go," Michael said.

"The girls are packing now."

"You can't pull the girls out of school."

"Who said anything about pulling them out of school? I said I'm leaving you."

The same hollow sensation that had rolled through his stomach this morning once again descended upon him. "I don't want you to take the girls away from their home."

"Okay, then you go."

"This is my house, too. Be reasonable. Let's talk this over."

"Hey, Mr. Special Agent, you're not listening," Jan said, her words drenched in sarcasm as she flicked her hand toward the scattering of photos that lay across the bed. "I've made up my mind. I'm leaving one way or the other."

Michael raised his voice. "Why won't you let me explain? You want me gone so bad, what is it you're trying to hide?"

The demand in his voice, the unexpected accusation caught Jan off guard. Michael saw the sudden fear in her eyes. Her glance darted to the left, away from his penetrating stare. Jan coughed and stepped back. Michael reached her and grabbed both her arms. "Speak to me. Are you having an affair?

In that instant, Jan's Alpha personality cracked. It was evidence enough she held a secret. She had lost control of the argument and hung her head. She was disoriented, unable to rebut. The unanticipated reference to her clandestine liaison rendered her mute.

"I love you, Jan. Are you going to throw it all away?"

Jan threw back her head and pulled back. "Let me go, she demanded.

Jan's guilty expression appeared and disappeared so quickly Michael might have missed it if he hadn't been looking directly at her face. But he knew—and so did she. "You ARE hiding something."

But Jan didn't have to answer. Gretchen appeared in the doorway, and Jan regained her self-control. "Mommy, I don't want to go." Gretchen's lower lip trembled.

"I told Tonya to help you pack. Now pack what you need for one night."

"Mommy, please. I don't want to go."

"I'll go," Michael said. "I want the girls to sleep in their own beds."

"No, daddy. I don't want you to go either." Gretchen ran to him and wrapped her arms around his waist.

"Gretchen," Jan ordered, "get in your room and get yourself packed."

"Just a minute, just a minute." Michael sat on the edge of the bed and lifted Gretchen into his arms. Gently he pulled wet strands of blonde hair from her tear-streaked cheeks and kissed her forehead.

"Sweetheart, let mommy and daddy worry about this. You're going to sleep in your own bed, like always. Nothing's going to happen to me. I'll be close by for you, okay?"

Gretchen nodded and touched her finger to his puffy lip. "Does it hurt?"

"Yes, but I'll get better. Promise."

Michael glanced at Jan. She was standing, arms folded, glaring as though he couldn't be trusted even while comforting his youngest daughter. As he sat holding Gretchen, Michael was hit with a tremendous pang of self-pity. It was as though all of his sins, shortcomings, broken promises, lapses in judgment and misdeeds had come due and payable at exactly the same hour.

"Let's get you to bed." He carried Gretchen toward the hall.

"Just leave, Michael. I'll put her in bed."

"Relax before you have a stroke. I'll put her in bed. It'll just take a minute."

Gretchen wasn't ready for bed, but Michael placed a pillow under her head, knelt beside her, and handed her a large stuffed parrot which she clutched with both arms.

"I love you, daddy," Gretchen said.

"I know, Sweetheart. I love you, too."

CHAPTER TWENTY-SEVEN

$

A S BECKY DROVE INTO Sugars' parking lot, the afternoon crowd was just arriving. Happy hour began at four. Fifty cents off well drinks and a smorgasbord of cold salami and stale chips was good enough reason for customers to duck out of the heat and take in the fine display of exposed breasts and seductive smiles. Sugars offered a tinge of excitement and a few moments of escape from the daily grind.

Becky knew the customers weren't drunk enough at this hour for their wallets to be sufficiently open. The afternoon stage talent was second-shelf, at best. Only when the sun went down, did Omar and Byron's best hit the stage. Becky knew that included her. Now she would have to perform. The days of skating through shifts by waiting tables were over.

Becky found Elaine in the dressing room considering an assortment of ear rings. "Elaine." Becky pulled up a chair beside Elaine and looked at her through the reflection in the mirror. "I'm going to dance tonight."

"That was the plan." Elaine held a ruby stud next to her ear and studied her reflection.

"I'm ready. No reservations. I'm ready to do it," Becky said.

"Omar will be so happy to know you're ready to work," Elaine said.

"I just needed to get my bearings, you know. Showing some skin won't kill me. You said so yourself. I need to make some money, so I made up my mind to do it. I never could have done it without your help." Becky's face lit up, the reflection of her caramel eyes swimming in the light.

"You haven't done it yet." Elaine was not overly enthused by Becky's exuberance. Rather, she was annoyed and changed the subject. "What happened to you yesterday morning?"

"I had to get home."

"When did you leave?"

"Around four-thirty, I think. I never said I was going to stay all night. I couldn't."

"So, you decided to leave your mess with me?"

"Mess? Elaine, I didn't think you needed me. He was sleeping and seemed all right."

"His name happens to be Michael, and he's a very fine and caring man."

"I thought you said he was like all the others," Becky replied.

"Yeah, well," Elaine turned and stared Becky down, "you don't worry about that. Got it? What I know is he stepped in for you, got his face pulverized, and you make a token gesture of help, then slip out in the middle of the night."

"I'm sorry. I appreciate what he did. I really do. Is he all right?"

Oh, he's getting along, thanks to me," Elaine said. "I spent all day yesterday taking him to the doctor and such. He's really a very considerate person, and brave, I might add."

"Good grief, Elaine, you can't be mad at me because I finally went home after a long night. I didn't do anything with him if that's what you think."

"Yeah, well, you better not."

"What's that supposed to mean?" Becky stood and backed away from the vanity. "You have a thing for him."

Elaine turned back toward the mirror and ignored the comment. "You better put on a great show tonight, and make my work count for something. Omar will hold it against me if you don't knock'um dead."

"Okay then, what should I wear?" Becky asked.

"Go with that business suit with the short skirt."

"Okay."

"And forget all about your knight in shining armor. You're done with him now. He's my customer."

"Sure, whatever you say, Elaine."

Elaine sat back and watched Becky change into her stage outfit. "I guess I do like him a bit," Elaine admitted. "I just wanted him to ask about me a bit while I was with him yesterday, and all I hear is about you all morning."

"What do you mean?"

"While I was taking him around to get doctored up, all he wanted to do was to ask me questions about you."

****

Since an hour before dusk, Cleet waited and watched the Cranfield home from his car. He parked along a row of thick hedges, near an intersection with a direct view diagonally across the street. He watched as a shiny four-door sedan flew up the drive and a woman and two kids hurried from the car. A short time later, Cranfield walked out the garage door with a suitcase in his hand. Cranfield backed down the drive as the garage door closed, Cleet's hand reached for the ignition key—but then, he stopped, and watched Cranfield drive away.

Cleet's gaze turned again toward the house and he looked it over closely, from the near gatepost to the far corner downspout. If Cranfield were leaving on a trip, he would be gone for a day or more. His wife and children would be alone and defenseless. As much as hurting Cranfield personally, Cleet wanted him rendered shocked and horrified. Cleet wanted Cranfield to experience the personal pain of having a loved one injured. Cleet's eyes widened as he studied the house. He was going to do it. The timing was perfect.

He retrieved a pair of cotton gloves, a roll of duct tape, and a carpet knife from under his seat. A security light cast a wide halo on the driveway. Cleet walked down the opposite sidewalk, and crossed the street at the far end of the Cranfield house. He kept to the shadows along a row of shrubs, found an open gate, and slipped into the backyard.

The sky was black with the narrow crescent moon low on the horizon. Still, Cleet felt exposed as though he were bathed in sunlight. He huddled near the ground and crept under the windows. At one window, thin rays of light peeked under the blinds. He grasped the brick casement and gingerly raised his head. A woman sat with her back to him, working at a desk. Even if he broke through the screen and glass, he could not reach her before she could flee. Besides, he wanted the children—it was the children Cleet wanted most.

He moved past the dark bathroom window, past half-drawn blinds of a patio door. At the last window, Cleet could see by an amber nightlight covered with a light green shade, two small forms asleep in their beds, adrift in Neverland, enjoying their dreams. What could he do to them? He could bind them and gag them. That would put Cranfield in a state of constant anxiety. Cleet thought about disfigurement, but quickly dismissed the idea. He didn't want to permanently maim any child. He just wanted them to be forever terrified of the dark.

A tiny fan oscillated between the foot of the children's beds inches in front of his nose. Cleet saw that the window was cracked open. He cut through the screen with the knife. With the screen removed, he retrieved a metal lawn chair from the patio and set it under the window. He placed his fingers under the window. Adrenaline coursed through his body. His mind hadn't been so clear in weeks. He would bind the children, arms and legs, tape their mouths, and lay a pillow over their faces. They would be able to breathe. They would also be forever terrified.

The instant the window began to move, an alarm blared from the rooftop with another yelping inside the house. Cleet stumbled from the chair, scrambled to his feet, and sprinted back to his car. He drove out of the neighborhood with his lights off. Sweat streamed from his forehead. He made it back to the freeway without being stopped.

Only when he was surrounded by an insulating cocoon of evening traffic did Cleet's breathing begin to slow. He was thankful he'd escaped, yet again filled with rage. The Cranfield's children would now be next to impossible to reach. Once the moved lawn chair and the cut window screen were discovered, the children would be guarded day and night.

Cleet figured he should wait until Cranfield returned, catch him at home and kill him in his front yard in front of his wife and kids. But that was too easy. Cleet wanted the man to suffer, to feel the emptiness of seeing a loved one lying injured and helpless. Cleet wanted Cranfield to experience real fear. When a man gets shot in the head he doesn't suffer. He just dies.

With nowhere else to go, Cleet drove to Bill

Raney's office. It was unlikely the accountant would be there, but as he pulled into the row of businesses, Cleet saw lights on in Raney's office. Cleet tried the front door and found it locked. He knocked on the door, then beat on it, then kicked at the base until he painfully whacked his toe.

"I know you're in there. Answer the door like a man."

If Raney was here, Cleet wanted to know if he had collected any money on his behalf to reduce his tax debt. If not, Cleet intended to give the numbers-crunching crook a dose of clarity. Raney had caused his tax problems; Raney was going to get him out of them.

Cleet retrieved a tire iron from his car trunk with the intent to jimmy open the door by bending back the aluminum frame. Maybe it would be easier to get in through the back door, he thought. Maybe Raney would respond after several good whacks to his SUV's windshield, the only car still in the back parking lot. Several tall cottonwoods blocked the glow of the moon on the back side of the office building. The back door was also locked.

As he turned, Cleet caught sight of a motionless form on the ground beside the passenger door of the SUV. For an instant, the form appeared shapeless, possibly a pile of rugs or a mound of dirt. In that brief moment of mental void, when reasoning and recognition have not yet joined, comes a split-second of doubt. Then, without blinking, Cleet realized he was looking at a dead body.

Cleet recoiled. He dropped the tire iron. A bolt of cold ran across his shoulders. Simultaneously, he felt in fear of his own life and repulsed by the fact he was standing near a dead man. Cleet peered into the darkness. He strained to hear so much as a cricket taking a shit. Only the gentle rustling of leaves in the summer breeze could be heard. He was alone with the body.

The sudden fright that had grabbed him slowly ebbed, and curiosity rose to replace it. Cleet was fairly sure who the dead man was, but he couldn't see. He had to roll the body over. Cleet stepped around the SUV and circled the corpse. The dead man's feet were under the vehicle. The sand and dirt that covered the lot was scattered. The passenger window was cracked. A violent struggle had happened right beside the passenger door.

Cleet kneeled, snagged the jacket collar with the tire iron, and pulled the body onto its back. It was Raney. The rising moon shone off of a bruised and puffy face. A cord was wrapped around his neck. His eyeballs bulged behind closed eyelids. For a few seconds, Cleet was transfixed, then he pulled away in disgust. An acidic taste filled his mouth. He felt slightly faint. He leaned against the back of the SUV with his hands on the bumper and threw up.

He knew he must leave, drive away, and forget what he saw. Cleet slipped around the edge of the building and to his car with the stealth of a burglar. Again, he was a block down the street before he turned on his headlights. Raney had it coming, he thought. He had it coming.

Cleet needed a rum and coke, maybe four or five. He would stop at the first bar he came to. Then again, maybe he didn't need a cocktail. It crossed his mind what he really needed, at the moment, was a full bottle of bourbon.

CHAPTER TWENTY-EIGHT

$

A S MICHAEL DROVE AWAY from his home, he was devastated. Someone had taken and mailed pictures of his battered face to Jan—pictures of him in bed with Elaine. Only one other person had been in the Elaine's house after the hotel fight the night before last. Only one person could have taken the photos. But even then, his thoughts focused on his wife. The photos weren't the real reason Jan threw him out. A convenient excuse, no doubt, but their marriage had been dying for months. His greatest concern was the effect the event had on his youngest daughter.

He would have to get a motel room for the night. But first, he drove to Sugars. If Crystal was there, he would confront her. Was this the thanks he got for defending her? Michael wanted to fill his chest with indignant rage over the pictures, but he couldn't. There was something about Crystal that made it impossible for him to hold onto any righteous anger. Besides, Jan had already sapped all outrage from his heart.

Michael didn't want to be seen in the club. He waited in the parking lot and kept his motor running. The night was warm, so he let the air conditioner hum to a Martina McBride CD of country melodies. He would wait until Crystal showed, even if it meant waiting until the bar closed.

Just past nine, she appeared and stuck a key into the door of a shiny blue Trans Am. Michael drove over and blocked her exit, then jumped from his car. "Crystal, I want to talk to you."

Michael was in front of her before she could unlock her door. He had her cornered. Having found her, he felt relief, but her body stiffened, her face tightened, her eyes expressed fear. Michael stepped back and tried to relax his posture. "I just want to talk."

"What do you want?"

"The pictures. You took them, right? My wife has already seen them. Why did you do that?"

Becky swallowed. "I'm sorry."

"Sorry says nothing. Why did you even take them?" Michael asked.

"Please forgive me. I didn't want to."

"Then why?" They were standing inches from each other, but Michael wasn't threatening. His tone was more curious than accusing. Michael waited for an answer that didn't come. "Is it because your real

212

name is Rebecca Dixon?"

Michael saw the shock in her eyes. Her mouth dropped open. For a moment, she couldn't respond. "Oh, I feel terrible," she said. "My father made me do it, but I know that's no excuse. He has it in for you. He wanted anything that had you in a compromised position."

Even with the absolute knowledge she had taken advantage of him, Michael felt more relieved than angry. Her confession was obviously sincere, her involvement apparently coerced. Her wet brown eyes reflected the overhead lights of the parking lot. The moon was up and the night smelled clean and cool.

"Would you like to take a walk?" he asked.

"No, I need to go."

"Just up to the corner and back.." She didn't answer immediately. "Please, I need to know a little more about the other night," he said.

Becky gazed into his eyes, wrestling with a simple decision. His whole eye socket was horribly black, but the texture of his words reassuring. Even so, she had no desire to talk to him at any length. His concerns were none of hers. He had wrecked her peaceful life once before. She wished nothing more than he would disappear. She didn't answer. "Just for a few minutes. It sure is a lovely night," Michael said.

Becky turned and stepped toward the street. "What do you want to know?"

"Let me park my car." Michael pulled his Acura into a line of other vehicles.

As he walked back to her, she was gazing

upward at the moon. Her face was scrubbed clean of stage makeup. She wore a pair of blue nylon jogging pants with a matching windbreaker.

"When did you know who I was?" she asked.

"As soon as I saw you in the lights of the hotel."

"Why didn't you say anything?"

"It didn't strike me as being any of my business why you worked at the club."

"But knowing who I was—why did you step in for me when that slug tried to pull me from the bedroom?"

"Why do you think?" Michael replied.

Becky looked at him as they walked. "I think you would have stepped in for either Elaine or Misty, too."

"There's a Dairy Queen," Michael pointed. "Would you like a treat?"

Becky shook her head. Michael let the idea drop. At the corner, they stopped under a streetlight facing each other. Michael wanted to touch her shoulders, to lift her chin with a gentle touch. But Becky did it for him. She lifted her face and gazed into his eyes.

"You said you had questions, but I already know what you want to ask," she said.

But then she said no more, and they both remained silent, gazing at each other. For Michael, all traffic stopped, and the locust in the trees fell silent. Void of makeup, Becky's face possessed a radiant glow that makeup could not enhance. Michael had witnessed her propriety and experienced her caring. At that moment, he saw a beauty more captivating than eyes alone could see.

Michael knew the cuteness of children and the charm of pretty girls. There were stunning women dressed in fashion, blessed with facial bones of striking structure. But charm and youth and features alone did not make any of them beautiful.

Michael beheld a woman who closely held the fires her heart contained. Michael saw a person of indefinable sweetness. A glint in her expressive eyes hinted she might one day release the love she held deep inside. Michael could tell Becky's heart was home to selfless charity and unbounded affection.

"I'm very sorry about your brother," Michael finally said. "Every day I wish I could have that morning back."

Becky listened, her gaze remained fixed on his face.

"Is he doing better?"

"He's doing better," she said. "I really hated you when that happened. Now, I get the feeling you're not the evil man I saw that morning. You didn't mean to shoot, Lance, did you?"

"No, I didn't mean for any of it to happen. I was careless and I'm very, very sorry."

"They had to take Lance in for a second surgery, but he's doing much better now," Becky said. "I'd rather not talk about it anymore."

"Your father is a very angry man, isn't he?" Michael asked.

Becky nodded and her eyes began to tear up.

"Please don't cry. I don't want to make you sad. I know I'm the biggest reason for your dad's hostility. But I was acting as a federal agent. If your dad tries to harm me, he'll be arrested and may go to jail. I don't want to see your family suffer anymore."

"I know, I've tried," Becky said. "He won't listen to reason. My mother passed away after a lengthy hospital stay and my father is terrified the same thing might happen to Lance. He's lost all perspective. It's as though Lance's injury gave him the excuse he'd been looking for—an excuse to blame the world for all his problems. I can't get through to him."

Tears now streamed down Becky's cheeks and she grabbed Michael's jacket lapels and pulled herself to his chest. The remorse she had shown when confronted with the pictures was a trickle of grief compared to the flood of anguish that spilled from her body.

"I'm pregnant, too, and my boyfriend left me." Becky sobbed. "He thinks I'm nothing but a stripper." Michael placed his hands on her shoulders, then he slipped his arms around her back and held her closely until the worst was over.

"Until tonight, I worked as a cocktail waitress. But I want to get away from my father so bad, earn my own money and move out of his house. Tonight, for the first time, I got on stage and stripped. It's so revolting." Becky succumbed to another wave of heartbreaking sobs. Michael held her gently while it passed. "I thought I could do it," she said, "but it makes me sick to be on stage. I'm so trapped. I'm so stuck." Becky's voice faded away.

What Michael had not understood until now was the coercion involved to make her work at Sugars.

If he could get her away from there, he would. Michael would not bring it up now, but he felt compelled to intervene. In the long run, places like Sugars did nothing for young women but use them up and spit them out, and harden them to life. Michael recognized his own participation in that cycle of exploitation and vowed to change.

"What do you want to do after you move away from your father?"

Becky released Michael's jacket and took a step back. A strange expression came over her face as though the question fell into the realm of prying. But she answered, "I want to have my baby and go back to school."

"That's good," he said. "Good for you."

Becky reached up and touched the edge of his lip. "I want you to know, I'm sorry now for getting you involved in a fight. I never should been at that hotel party, but I was glad you were there."

"We all do things we regret," Michael said. "I regret what happened to your brother, but I take responsibility for it."

For a while longer, they stood facing each other in silence on the street corner.

Finally, Becky spoke. "I appreciate you listening to my problems. You didn't have to." Her voice took on a more businesslike tone. "I told you about the pictures. I'm not proud of having taken them and if I had to do it over, I wouldn't. But we don't have anything else to talk about."

She turned to leave. "Thank you for the walk. I needed that, but please leave me alone. The way I see things, you're part of the problems I've had lately, and I've told you about my father. I can handle myself from here on out. We've said all we need to say to each other." And with that, Becky headed back up the sidewalk toward the parking lot.

Michael found himself leaning against the light pole, caught short with nothing to say, as he watched her walk away.

CHAPTER TWENTY-NINE

$

WHEN BECKY GOT HOME, she went straight to bed. She struggled, without success, to dismiss the shameful display she had performed at the club, hopeful her mind would escape into the unconscious refuge of sleep. It was not to be. Her conversation with Michael had her wide awake. She stared at the gray shadows cast upon the ceiling by the moonlight through the blinds. He was just an unpleasant memory, she told herself. Her unborn baby, her brother, and her father were the important people in her life. Becky rolled onto her side and tried to relax her exhausted body and drift into dreamland. But all she felt were the places on her arms and back where Michael had held her while she cried into his shirt.

Shortly after midnight, the front door banged open. Becky heard her father stumble into the house, crash into a floor lamp, and send it flying across the room. Becky ran from her bedroom to the head of the stairs. Cleet staggered around the first floor. He flailed at the sheet music on the piano, sent it airborne, then fell over the arm of the couch and dropped into a heap on the floor beside it.

Becky waited. Her father's form remained still, so she went down and closed the front door. She moved the coffee table aside and pulled his feet so that he was stretched out on the floor. Her father reeked of liquor. Becky removed his shoes and knelt beside him. "It's going to all right, daddy. It's going to be all right." She tucked a couch pillow under his head and kissed him on the cheek.

****

Michael drove aimlessly around Dallas. A hollowness settled in his chest accompanied with despair and self-pity. Everything he'd worked for or cared about was crumbling at his feet..

Finally, he stopped and checked into a second class motel along Garland Road. He quickly discovered the room was neither what his tired body needed nor what he expected. The neon sign over the motel office appeared modern, the vehicles in the parking lot looked respectable. At first glance, the room appeared clean and the mattress was firm. But the toilet wouldn't flush and Michael spied a used condom behind it. He dismissed the sight because he didn't have the energy to contemplate its disgusting implications beyond the notion that the maid didn't want to deal with it either.

He inspected the sheets before he climbed into

bed. He could live with what he saw though they looked more dingy than white. The blanket was as cozy as a layer of tissue paper, and he heard every grunt and groan of his next-door neighbors as they tried to snap their bed springs into the wee hours of the night.

He lay in the bed, wide awake, staring into the darkness. Getting fired hadn't come as a surprise. The conversation with Becky Dixon had soothed his beleaguered mind though it provided more questions than answers. Holding her while she cried about her unborn baby and her irrational father had Michael pleasantly confused. She had confided in him. She had placed her face on his chest and remained there as he wrapped his arms about her. In the last twenty-four hours his life had been shattered in many ways. Yet as he lay in the darkness listening to auto traffic roll by on the street, Michael's mind found peace, the vacant feeling left his chest, and he fell into a deep sleep.

The next morning, Michael found an acceptable apartment complex and placed a deposit on a one bedroom loft. It occurred to him that Jan's dismissal and insistence he move out was too abrupt, final, and extremely convenient. Yes, she saw pictures of him in bed with a strange woman. But he was fully clothed, his face was beat up, and she didn't give him the least little chance to explain. She was glad the pictures showed up so she didn't have to make up another excuse to get him out.

The change in his wife had been building for months. She must be having an affair? She certainly had plenty of chances to meet other men—other

Realtors or clients. During last night's argument, he knew he had caught her concealing a secret,

Well, he was a trained investigator. He'd tracked down money hidden from the IRS and arrested purveyors of dubious tax shelters who preyed on unsophisticated investors. Currently, he didn't have a job, so he had time to investigate his own wife. He'd start with the colleagues in her office. He'd play the role of home buyer and get one of them to talk. If she wanted to be rid of him, so be it. But he'd find out what she was hiding if it was the last thing he ever did.

He wandered west on Northwest Highway and realized he was within blocks of Elaine's townhouse. It wouldn't hurt to stop by and thank her for her help after the incident. She had gotten him into that mess, but she had done her best to help him through the unfortunate outcome.

Elaine answered the door wrapped in a fuzzy, lime-green robe. Her smudged eyeliner made her look like a sleepy panda. Before she spoke, her vision was layered in a mental fog, her expression a combination of confusion and contempt. The instant she recognized Michael a measure of warmth brightened her eyes. Her rehearsed club smile appeared, her shoulders relaxed, and a touch of friendliness settled across her countenance. Still, the effort seemed to make her face crack.

"Michael, you came to see me."

"Did I wake you?"

"No, what time is it?"

"A little past noon."

Elaine stretched her arms to the sky and yawned

until Michael could see the dental work in her upper molars. She shook her head and a genuine smile curled her lips as fresh blood reached her brain.

"It's time to get up anyway. Come in, won't you? I'll make some tea."

Michael followed her into the apartment. He had gotten to know Elaine because of the simple need for companionship. Even if it included a visual tease, talking with Elaine soothed the pressure in his life and eased his mind. Elaine addressed him by his first name and treated him like a friend. What was wrong with having a platonic friend who made him laugh?

But any future with Elaine was anchored in wet putty. He wasn't going to ask her age, but twenty-five had to be in the rear view mirror. She had been working in places like Sugars for too long. The nightly grind was getting to her looks, and Michael knew most of the phrases she cooed to him were canned and rehearsed. Never-the-less, he needed her friendly face on this morning and to hear her talk of bright tomorrows even if the rosy lies were spoken for money.

Elaine microwaved two cups of water, then placed a tea bag in each. They waited, assessing each other as the tea steeped. Elaine lit a cigarette and scooted closer to Michael.

"It's nice to see you first thing in the morning," she said.

"I was driving around. Thought I'd see if you were here. I wanted to thank you for helping me to the doctor."

"Oh, Michael, it was the least I could do."

"And I've always enjoyed your company," he said. Michael stirred his hot tea and took a sip.

She touched his hand. "Your eye looks dreadful, but I can see it's healing." His shiner had morphed from blue-black to a sallow green with purple highlights.

Michael shrugged. "My wife left me. She kicked me out last night."

"Oh. Michael, I'm so sorry. It wasn't because of me, was it?"

"No, we've been having problems for some time."

Elaine ran her hand down his neck. "What can I do to help?"

Michael looked at Elaine more closely. Away from the glitzy dance lights, garish makeup, and seductive costumes, she appeared worn and senescent. Michael dropped his gaze and felt her touch. In spite of her just-out-of-bed appearance, she represented human companionship. Elaine was one person happy to see him.

"I'm glad you were home and let me in."

"Michael, I'll always let you in." Elaine slipped her other hand to the far side of his face. "Kiss me, Michael."

He let her fingers guide his face to hers. Their lips brushed. She pulled his mouth firmly to hers and the bitter licorice tinge of tobacco breath bit his tongue. Elaine ran her fingers through his hair. Her nails scraped his scalp with an invigorating tingle. Michael reached for her thinly clad body and pulled her to himself.

He held her and inhaled her female scent.

Holding Elaine made everything feel better, but only for a moment. The woman in his arms was not the woman he had known for the past twelve years. Elaine's enthusiasm made his sore lip throb, and try as he might, sex was not within his ability on this morning. As much as he liked Elaine, Michael now wished he hadn't knocked on her door. Michael released her and backed away.

"Slow down. Can't we just talk?"

"Michael, come here."

"I can't. With all I've been though, I just can't."

"I need you." Elaine opened her robe and exposed her breasts as though she were giving them only to him. These were the same breasts he'd already seen as often as his car keys. "Come and touch me," she pleaded.

"Elaine, please. Take a shower and get dressed, and I'll take you to lunch."

Elaine stood in front of him with her robe open. The most forlorn expression descended upon her face. Every feature of her face began to crinkle as if subjected to excruciating pain, and Michael could see she was about to burst into tears.

"Michael, help me. I need you. Please."

He stepped to her, closed her robe, and kissed her on the forehead. "Maybe I'd better go."

Elaine nuzzled her cheek against his neck. "You don't have to. Would you just hold me for a little while?"

Michael led her to the couch and let her sit in his lap. He put his arms around her and they quietly sat there until they were napping in each other's arms.

A suffocating weight on his chest forced Michael awake. Elaine was on top of him, her breath drifting across his face. He could see a clock on the bookshelf, but couldn't read the time. He rolled himself out from under Elaine. Her limp elbow popped him across his sore jaw,

It was almost 4 P.M. Elaine had probably gotten to bed about dawn. She needed every extra hour of sleep to be ready to face another night of dancing and carousing. He gently shook her awake.

"Don't you have to work?"

"What time is it?" she asked.

"Almost four."

"Yeah, got to go in." Elaine sat up, shook her head, and massaged her temples. "Be a darling and call Byron. Tell him I'm running a bit late, but I'm on my way." Then, without another word, she pointed herself toward the bathroom.

Michael called Byron at the club, then let himself out. As he drove toward Addison looking for another hotel, Michael realized his relationship with Elaine had gone too far. Today was the second time she had come on to him. He didn't see her in a romantic light. He felt sorry for her and wanted life to hand her a winning lottery ticket. But he wasn't it. He knew he couldn't fulfill her physical desires or romantic hopes. The last two days made his situation crystal clear. His life had hit rock bottom on all fronts. If he was to have a productive and meaningful future, everything would have to start anew.

CHAPTER THIRTY

$

CLEET AWOKE ON HIS LIVING ROOM FLOOR, disoriented and achy. He was stuck to his clothes in a clammy sweat with a bladder ready to explode. He stumbled to the hall bathroom and stood over the toilet the better part of five minutes. He drank a quart of water from the faucet using his hands as a cup, and grabbed a towel to wipe the sweat from his face and the slobber from his chin. When Cleet returned to the living room, Becky was coming down the staircase.

"I wanted to wait until you got up," she said, "before I left the house."

Without a word, Cleet fell into a recliner and closed his eyes.

"He knows who I am," Becky said.

Cleet struggled to open his eyes. "Who?"

"The IRS agent, that's who. You already mailed out those photos, didn't you. Well, his wife saw them, and she kicked him out of their house. He confronted me about them. I hope you're satisfied."

A smile cracked across Cleet's pasty white face.

"Why are you so devious?" Becky raised her voice. "Look at you. What were you doing last night?"

Cleet shook his head. The thought of what he saw last night made him shudder, but he said nothing.

"Fine—get yourself arrested for driving drunk," Becky said. "I just hope you don't do something really stupid."

Cleet remained smug and silent.

Becky took a deep breath and stared at her father. "I've got to go. I have classes this morning and a doctor's appointment this afternoon. Then I work until eleven."

"So, why are you going back if he knows who you are?" Cleet asked.

"Because I'm supposed to be there."

"I thought you hated the place?"

"I do. It's disgusting. But, I can make more money there than anywhere else, and that's what I'm going to do."

Cleet cocked his head in the direction of his daughter's rising voice. His eyelids slit open a fraction. By sheer will, he was trying to suppress the dull throb in his skull, but her tone tugged at his attention. "What are you saying?"

"I'm going to make enough money to move out of here. That's what I'm saying. I'm going to get away from you."

"Ha! Talk about acting stupid. You'll never finish school without me, and you can't afford to have that bastard baby without my insurance."

The hurtful, unfiltered words hit Becky like a slap in the face. She swallowed and blinked back a threatened onslaught of tears. Across the room her eyes focused on a large watercolor print hanging above the piano. A fisherman sat in a rowboat drifting across a pond of blue. The man and the boat were dwarfed by a cliff arrayed in a smattering of reds, and yellows, and browns. Becky's thoughts drifted to the rowboat and nestled beside the tiny figure with his pole in the water. The air was calm, quiet, and serene.

Cleet sat forward on the recliner. "If you want to see that son-of-a-bitch so bad, you can start up a conversation with him. Tell him you're sorry about the pictures. Ask him if he'd give you a ride up north so you can leave your car at the club for one of the other girls.

"I didn't say anything about seeing him again. You don't listen. You never listen."

Ask him to take you to the Crestview Townhouses near Parkway and Beltline. You know where that is. There's a construction site on the backside of the property. Just call and let me know when. I'll be waiting and I'll have a little heart-to-heart talk with the guy."

"He probably won't even be there today."

"Yeah, yeah, I know. But whenever he shows, ask for the ride, and give me a call. He'll do it for a sweet thing like you."

"You're absolutely out of your mind. I'm not helping anymore with your sick schemes."

"Dammit, Rebecca. I'm not asking, I'm telling you." Cleet stood and clenched his fist. "After what he did to Lance, I want a piece of him."

Becky could only shake her head and fight to choke back tears that ran down her cheeks. "I don't understand what's happened to you." The words caught in her throat. "I have to go."

Once she arrived at Sugars, Elaine yanked Becky from her thoughts and cornered her the moment she walked into the dressing room.

"I thought I told you to stay away from him."

Becky stared into a tight, pinched face. "He came to me, cut me off in the parking lot last night. I wasn't looking for him."

Well, Misty saw the whole thing. She said you went down the street with him talking like old pals. That don't sound like you were trying to get away from him."

"I tried to warn him. My father is out to hurt him."

"I don't get it," Elaine said, "but I better or I'll give you what he got and mess up your pretty little face."

"He's an IRS agent and he shot my brother."

Elaine's brain took an instant to process the information. "What? Did he kill him?"

"No, but he's still in the hospital."

"So—so, you've been stalking him. Is that it?" Elaine was livid.

Becky stood mute, but she could see—Elaine's brain was in high gear, trying to make sense of new information. "You found out he came around the club. That's why you came in here looking for a job."

Elaine stepped closer and pinned Becky against a vanity bench with a knuckle to her chest. "You conniving bitch. I knew you didn't know shit, afraid of your own shadow. And I tried to help you. You're messing with poison, you mess with me. And to think he defended you. You ungrateful bitch."

Becky coughed and grabbed her chest, but managed to remain standing. "It's not what you think. My dad has it in for him. He's in danger."

"I'll tell him." Elaine said, "but I don't believe you."

"I told him myself, but I don't think he took it seriously."

"Why should he? Every other thing you say is a lie."

"You don't know my father, Elaine. He's out of control."

"I'm warning you for the last time," Elaine said. "I see you around him again, I'll make you wish you'd never laid eyes on me." With that, Elaine pushed Becky against the table until her shoulders hit the mirror.

Left alone, Becky regained her composure and dressed in a costume consisting of an emerald green skirt with a matching jacket over a florid red bra and panties. She was to go on stage in thirty minutes. She took a drink tray from the bar and cleared off a few tables as she assessed the customers. The main floor was recessed in deep shadows. Speakers hung high in the ceiling pulsated with a heavy beat as Tina Turner warbled above the din of conversations and laughter.

As she picked up some empty glasses, a voice called from behind her. "Could you bring me another?"

Becky turned. "Sure, what are you having?"

"Another margarita, Crystal, would be great."

Her body stiffened. She peered into the shadows. "Why are you here? Don't you think I have enough to deal with?"

"I just wanted to have a drink," Michael said.

"I don't believe you. I told you, we're through talking. Go have your drink somewhere else."

"I didn't mean to upset you."

"Well, you are. I have nothing more to say to you. I've told you to steer clear of my father, but if you think I'm going to tell you anything more about him, you're badly mistaken."

"I'm not here to ask any questions," he said.

"But you are here, aren't you? Why?"

The question hung in the air. Becky glared at him, an angry sadness welling up in her eyes. The verbal thrashing she'd received from her father and the physical confrontation with Elaine had frazzled her emotions. Her resolve to move ahead was on the verge of collapse. She couldn't take any more, especially not from him. She wanted someone to hold her, someone to tell her that soon everything would be all right. More lies, threats, or manipulations were going to push her to the breaking point.

"You thought you'd wait around to see me dance, didn't you? Well, here I am. See me?" She pulled open her green jacket. "Are you getting an eyeful? I can dance for you right here if you want me to." Becky stuck her finger in her mouth in mock seduction and thrust her breasts across the table. "Do you see me now?"

"I'm sorry, I'll go," Michael said as he got up from the table and walked out of Sugars.

****

After Becky left the house, Cleet made himself an ice pack and lay on the couch trying to stem the throbbing of a massive hangover. By mid-afternoon he was hungry and still nauseous, praying the tomato juice he drank would stay down. When his cell phone rang it sounded like a fire alarm going off next to his ear.

"Dixon." The voice was unfamiliar.

"Yes."

"You've been sticking your nose where it don't belong."

It wasn't who Cleet thought it might be. The caller's tone forced him to sit up and focus his foggy mind. "Who is this?"

"Never mind who this is. Just listen up, and listen good. We've been watching you. Don't you have a business to run? Why aren't you at your office? You've caused enough trouble. You better start minding your own business and quit staying out past your bedtime." With that the line went dead.

At first, the subtle threats made no sense, but Cleet's brain made it's own deductions in spite of his stupor. Numerous possible explanations emerged. Was that police detective Collins or one of his men following him? Had someone seen him around the Cranfield's home? Had his car been spotted at Raney's office? Maybe it was something else entirely—a disgruntled employee or an unsatisfied customer. Cleet couldn't think straight. As he set the cell phone on the coffee table he had every intention of taking a shower and leaving the house. But as soon as he reclined back on the couch, he once again fell asleep.

****

That night, Becky didn't bother to go home. She paid a hundred dollars for a motel room in North Dallas to be alone, to be away from her father. She slept until housekeeping called, showered and dressed, and sat on the edge of the bed until the maid actually took over the room. Becky knew she was going back to the club, but she walked to her car with the enthusiasm of a condemned woman forced to tie her own noose.

She would keep a personal promise to herself. She would do whatever it took to gain her personal and financial freedom, however distasteful the journey might be. Yesterday, she was thankful she'd been able to run Michael out of the club.

Seeing him there had been the final straw in an ever increasing day of stress. She just couldn't get on stage and remove her clothes if he were there. She had learned how to detach her mind from her body while she danced in front of total strangers. But her will turned to mush at the thought of dancing half-nude in front of him. She just couldn't.

She knew he was a number of years older than she, but it was the maturity he displayed that drew her to him. He had faults, she was well aware of that, but he was caring and affectionate in spite of his own troubles. But now, she might never see him again. Her future was entirely in her own hands.

Becky drove south on Greenville Avenue toward Sugars. She knew she should turn around and get as far away from the club as possible and its den of lecherous stares and lewd applause. But she had made a promise to herself, she had to go on. At this moment in her life, it was the only option she had.

CHAPTER THIRTY-ONE

$

CLEET MILLED AROUND THE HOUSE with his fourth cup of coffee, completely unaware Becky was not in her room. Paternal thoughts of Lance's recovery occupied little more than a tiny corner of his mind. His focus was on agent Cranfield, because today he could pick up the gun he bought.

Tonight would be the night. Becky would be at the club. If Cranfield didn't come by, Cleet thought she would know how to find him. He would talk with her before evening and review his plan—the construction site behind Crestview Townhouses after dark. Cleet would promise Becky anything to get Cranfield to that secluded site. He could get funds from his company, more than enough to sway her sympathies. She wanted financial freedom.

Cleet would make it all possible.

He had his mind made up. He got in his car and squealed from the driveway. Since he had already paid for the gun, he could spend his last few dollars on a box of bullets, which he did. As soon as he got back in the car, he called Becky.

"Why are you calling?" she answered.

"Where are you?"

"I'm headed to work. I have to work today."

"Fine," Cleet said. Her tone sounded like she was ready for an argument, but he no longer had any interest in how she spent her time. He wanted only one thing from his daughter, and he was ready to tell her every lie in the book to get her to comply. "Have you seen that IRS agent?"

"No, I haven't."

"I want you to call me if you see him at the club."

"No, forget it. I told you no. I'm done helping you conspire against him."

"Why are you protecting a worthless coward?"

"Because you're wrong."

"Listen." Cleet was breathless, his body so pumped he could hardly speak and drive at the same time. "Find him for me, and I'll give you the money to find your own place. $10,000 to start. When its time to have your baby you can use the family insurance. I'll give you another $10,000 then so you can have a new start without working at that place anymore."

"I don't know where he is."

"Just find him, then give me a call. Ask around. Have him give you a ride to Crestview, like I said, after your shift is over."

"What do you intend to do?"

"Make him face me like a man, that's all. I want him to stand up without all the official bullshit running interference for him."

"He's already beat up, or didn't you notice in the pictures. Why can't you let that be his punishment?"

"Rebecca, do you want the money or not? I want him to face me."

"I'll think about it, but I wish you'd let it go," Becky said. "I have to hang up now."

****

Michael stared at another motel room ceiling knowing he wasn't going to accept Barnes' offer to transfer to another department. A good part of the day would be needed to move into his new apartment, and then he'd take a few days off before he tried to find out what Jan was hiding and look for a new job.

Of all the disappointments he endured over the last few days, including life-changing pronouncements that knocked the wind out of him like a punch to the gut, Becky Dixon's rebuke at the club hurt the most. Hadn't he defended her at the hotel? Hadn't he been reasonable when he confronted her about the photographs? Wasn't he sympathetic when she explained how she'd been coerced into working at Sugars in the first place?

Maybe she was uncomfortable with the entire thought of him. He would never be able to change the fact that he shot her brother. But to blow up in his face without warning because he was in the club and wanted a drink. Didn't he deserve better?

Michael drove home and let himself in the back door. Jan had agreed that he could get his things while she and the girls were gone. He walked the halls, glanced in the rooms. The house was no more silent than when he lived there. The house hadn't been his home for sometime. It was just another motel room that happened to have pictures of people he knew hanging on the walls.

It was late afternoon when he finished moving his personal items and had enough furniture in the loft apartment to call it home base. The image of Becky resurfaced in his mind like a continuous video clip that would not end. She had an inner resolve for such a young woman, and yet a sensitivity and vulnerability that couldn't be hidden. He had to speak with her again. The leisurely walk the other evening could not be left to a one time encounter. Those few minutes seemed so right. He had never felt more connected to another person as when he held her while she cried.

****

When Becky got to Sugars, she immediately sought out Elaine. "Where can I find Michael?"

"I thought I told you to stay away from him," Elaine said.

"I have to see him today."

"You need to get ready to work and forget about him."

Becky persisted. "Elaine, tell me what you know. When does he come in? Do you think he'll be here today?"

Elaine's eyes narrowed as she stepped closer to Becky. "You had a little spat with him out front yesterday, didn't you?" Amber saw it and told me. "What was that all about?"

"Well," Becky tried to chose the right words, "I already told him I didn't want to see him anymore. That's what you wanted and that's what I wanted. But the first chance he gets he orders a drink and wants to strike up a conversation."

"That's what we do for customers around here, you know. We dance for them and we serve drinks."

"He's different. He shot my brother."

"He's still a customer."

"But there's more to it, and I've told you. My father means him harm. I can't get my father to calm down. The best thing for Michael is to stay away from here."

"Whatever," Elaine scoffed. "You're exaggerating. He's a federal agent with a gun. Your dad messes with him, and it'll be your dad in the morgue."

"Please, Elaine, listen to me. He's in danger. I have to see him."

"No—you listen to me. He's my customer, and you'd better steer clear of him. You think that just because you're as fresh as a budding flower you can horn in on the good men around here. Well, let me clue you in you prissy little slut, you ain't no better than the rest of us. You want to keep working around here, you better quit messing with other girls' regulars."

"I'm trying to tell you he's in danger."

"Michael's a big boy. He can take care of himself."

"Not if he doesn't know the threat. My father is capable of anything in his current state of mind."

Becky turned and walked to the other side of the dressing room to the laughter of Elaine and several of the other girls. Elaine was no help.

Just yesterday, Becky had seen him. Right here in the club, she had insulted Michael and run him off. Told him she never wanted to see him again, and she kept telling herself she didn't. During every waking hour, her father's rage had not subsided. In all the time since Lance's shooting, Becky prayed her father would come to his senses. She now sensed her father was about to do something he would forever regret.

She would do whatever it took to get her father help, but first she had to find Michael. In all likelihood, her father was looking for him, too. Her best chance to keep the two men from meeting, she realized, was to contact her father and get him to the construction site he mentioned. Then she would have time to find Michael and warn him in no uncertain terms. She snapped on a pair of sunglasses and flew out the side door with Elaine hollering after her, "and don't ever come back."

As she approached her car, Becky heard Michael's voice. "Becky."

She spun around. An incredulous expression of shock crossed her face, and then relief. A wave of emotion, of something approaching joy, swelled through her body.

"Can we talk?" Michael asked.

They stood silently facing each other. The sun was falling to the west, but the day was still hot. Heat thermals shimmered above the asphalt. Windshields, now glaring reflectors, hurled blinding shard of light across the parking lot.

"My father is out to get you," she said, "He's lost all sense of reality. He's not going to rest until you are seriously hurt."

"Oh well," Michael said, "this hasn't been my week. One more thing can't make it any worse."

Becky looked at him as if he'd lost his mind. "I'm serious. My father blames you for all of his financial problems. He means to hurt you in every way he can."

"Too late," Michael shrugged. "I don't work for the government anymore. I got fired."

"That's terrible."

"Not really. Once I thought it over, I figured it was the best thing that could have happened."

"Still, my father still blames you for all of his troubles. You're the scapegoat for all the sins of society."

"It can't be that bad," Michael protested.

"You don't know my father and all he's been through. He's been seething and plotting. He called me this morning to get . . ."

Becky saw a flurry of movement between two cars right before the profile of a handgun flashed before her eyes. A glint of sunlight reflected from polished metal. A microsecond later came a loud pop and a thud. A bullet peeled back a piece of car fender like the lid to a sardine can. A second shot came immediately after with the sound of a hollow whop as though someone had smacked a side of beef with a baseball bat. An incredible expression of shock appeared on Michael's face. Even before he grabbed his stomach, a dark red stain spread over his white shirt above his belt.

When Michael looked up, his eyes were wide with disbelief. He began to teeter and fell to one knee. A second later, he tipped over and dropped to the pavement. He rolled over, flat on his back on the hot asphalt. The sun was nothing more than a yellow blur a million miles away. Then there was shade. Cleet Dixon stood over him, his huge body blocked the rays of the sun.

"Daddy, STOP," Becky screamed.

Cleet kicked at Michael's feet so that his wobbly legs fell off the tottering support of his heels. Cleet checked Michael's jacket for a weapon. Michael was unarmed.

"It's not like me to shoot an unarmed man," Cleet said, "but when there's scum in the streets—." Cleet circled Michael's prostrate body. His fingers massaged the gun's hand grip. He didn't need to cock his gun, just point and pull the trigger.

Becky slugged her father in the back with no effect. Cleet continued to circle his prone victim. Cleet enjoyed the sight, Michael's contorted face and agonizing moans. A number of customers were in the parking lot witnessing events unfold. They kept their distance kneeling behind parked cars.

Cleet could shoot him in the head and be done

with it. A shot from a .22 at this range would be lethal. The police would come and haul him away and that would be the end of it. But the satisfaction of euphoric revenge would be with him forever.

If he shot him again in the stomach, it would be true justice. It would probably kill him, but not immediately. He would suffer as Lance suffered. Cleet considered his next move. The sight of the man writhing on the hot, filthy asphalt made him giddy. A rush of sexual tension exploded through his body and Cleet roared with laughter.

"Daddy!" Becky cried. She threw her pocketbook at him, but missed. "Don't do it."

The flying purse brought Cleet's head around. "Some people just don't deserve to live, Sweetie." Cleet leaned over, jammed the gun barrel into Michael's side, and began a slow squeeze on the trigger.

A bang split the sweltering heat like a thunderclap. The hot air held its breath. Cleet Dixon staggered backward. Becky dropped to her knees and watched in horror as the sight unfolded before her like a scene in a horrible dream.

Blood bubbled from a hole near Cleet's neck. He stumbled, cantilevered backward in a series of quick, unsteady steps until he crashed into a parked car, the gun fell from his hand, his knees gave way, and he crumbled into a heap.

"Becky," the name gurgled from his throat.

"Daddy." Becky forced herself to stand. Cleet rolled onto his back, grasping his throat as red oozed through his fingers. His mouth was open. A drowning gurgle rolled up from his lungs. Becky ran toward him and dropped on her knees beside him. "Oh, daddy," she cried. Cleet's mouth was full of blood. He was gurgling and choking. Becky glanced around and screamed. "Help me turn him over. He's drowning in his own blood. Please. Please."

Cleet's twitching feet creased to move. Becky turned his head as blood ran from his mouth onto the asphalt. Cleet's gurgling diminished into little more than bubbles forming on his lips, and Becky knew. "Goodbye, daddy. I love you."

She saw Michael in the corner of her eye, groaning louder, blood still oozing through his fingers as he tried to sit up. In that instant, the allegiance of a loving daughter disappeared and concern for another injured man took hold. Asked to explain her actions, Becky would have been unable to do so, but she dashed to Michael's side. Without a second thought, the injury of this virtual stranger consumed her attention. She pressed his jacket against his wound. Michael raised his hand ever so slightly. Becky took it and brought it to her cheek.

"Don't talk, don't talk. I'm here. You're going to be all right."

Fifteen feet away, Cleet Dixon's dilated pupils stared directly at the sun. His crooked jaw and distended tongue struggled for one last breath that had already come. A bystander brought over a windshield visor and placed it over his face.

"Someone call an ambulance," Becky pleaded to the assembling crowd.

"I already have," came a voice.

Becky looked up into the unfamiliar face of a stocky, middle-aged man in a worn business suit who walked up. The man knelt beside Becky and Michael.

"EMS will be here any minute," the man said. "Hang in there, Cranfield."

"Frank?"

"Yeah, Cranfield. It's me."

Someone knelt down on the other side of Michael, pulled back the saturated business jacket, and placed a towel over the bleeding. Becky held his hand listening as a siren wailed in the distance. "You're going to be all right," she said.

The ambulance made its way through the lot. A medical team strapped Michael to a gurney and loaded him in the back of the ambulance.

"I'm going with you," Becky said as she clung to Michael's hand. She remained beside him until he was rolled into the emergency room. Then she was alone. Her hands were covered in blood, her knees cut and bleeding where she scrapped them on the asphalt. She collapsed into a waiting room chair, and dropped her head as she offered up a silent prayer.

CHAPTER THIRTY-TWO

$

SEVERAL DAYS LATER, Michael lay in his hospital bed reading another 'Get Well' card. Flower arrangements sent by co-workers and neighbors crowded every flat surface. Becky threw open the curtains and afternoon sunlight poured into the room. She came to his room every day. Lance was still in the hospital. Becky said she thought visiting Michael was the proper thing to do since she was there anyway.

A light rap came at the door. Frank pushed it open, a sports magazine rolled in his hand.

"Looks like you're feeling pretty good," Frank said.

Doctor says I'll be good as new in a week with a nice scar to forever remind me of Monday.

Frank nodded. "That's good to hear. This is hot

off the newsstand." Frank handed Michael the magazine. "I thought you might want to read up on the Cowboys and the upcoming season."

"Thanks."

"So, you're not coming back downtown?"

"No. After Barnes let me go and I thought about it, I'd say he did me a big favor. I'll have to thank him sometime."

"I just figured, with all your time in grade, you'd want to work out something, you know, for benefit and retirement purposes."

"Going in a different direction, Frank. I'm going to take a look at what else is out there. Besides, Barnes might have been right. Maybe I wasn't cut out for that line of work. Anyway, I've had enough of being a tax collector. I've done my tour. On the other hand, you have what it takes, Frank. The Service needs honest, hard working agents like you."

Frank replied with a simple nod.

Michael reached his hand out from the bed. "I'll always be in your debt, Frank. Not only did you save my life, you gave me a new lease on life." Frank took Michael's hand and squeezed it.

"I'd been following him for a few days," Frank said. "After what happened at the house and the threats he'd made, I knew he was up to no good. He hadn't been going to work and I found out he bought a gun. I'm just glad I was there at the right time." Frank glanced at Becky who set her book aside. "I know this is a sad subject, but I may as well let you both know. The police are pretty sure he killed his accountant, a guy named William

Raney. He was found strangled behind his office. Dixon's fingerprints were all over the victim's vehicle and back door."

Becky listened with detached interest. Frank spoke of details she might as well know, but details that held no relevance for her future. Her father was gone. She couldn't think of anything she might have done to save him. She knew she wasn't to blame. She had attended his funeral and buried him next to her mother. It was where he always wanted to be. His emotional suffering was over.

"Anyway, I wanted to come by and wish you a quick recovery," Frank said.

"Keep in touch, Frank. Thanks for coming by."

Frank Masters walked down the hospital corridor, free from all suspicion, a hero by some accounts. Frank was ready to recommit himself to the daily toil of feeding the United States Treasury. Now he'd killed three men, one in the line of duty, one in self-defense to save a colleague, and one he'd murdered, pure and simple. He would never breathe a word of it. Would he dare entangle himself with another shady accountant? Frank was a greedy man, but he wasn't stupid. A lot of grass would grow under his feet before he ever entered a similar arrangement. In the meantime, Frank would fulfill his duties, meet his quotas, keep Barnes happy with cases closed and taxes collected. Frank Masters a federal Special Agent—a killer with a badge and a gun.

After Frank left the room, Becky came to the side of the bed.

"I'm so sorry for what happened," Michael said.

"It's over and in the past," Becky said. "I'd like to leave it that way."

"I sure appreciate you coming to see me everyday," Michael said.

Becky gazed down at him. "Something deep inside tells me you're a wonderful man. It's the least I could do."

"I can be there for you and the baby if you'll let me."

Becky swallowed and reached for his hand. Those were the words she wanted to hear, needed to hear. Michael's words meant a lot. They provided the emotional support she needed to deal with the new life growing within her body.

"Someday I hope Lance will forgive me as you have and give me a second chance."

Becky dabbed her eyes with tissues from the night stand. "Just give him some time. He doesn't care to hear your name right now, but he's a very resilient and fair minded kid. And personable, too. In time he'll forgive you. I know he will."

"Jan, my wife, called when you were visiting Lance. She said she'd come and bring the girls tomorrow."

"I'd love to meet your daughters."

"I want you to, and you will. Tonya and Gretchen. They're smart and pretty and do very well in school."

At that moment, Jan was with clients. Liz was at the Cranfield house watching the girls. Right after the shootings in the club parking lot, Jan filed for divorce. In time, Liz became the girls regular nanny. The girls adored her. Jan helped Liz get a larger apartment and paid half of the monthly lease. She gave Liz a handsome raise. Jan would do almost anything for Liz.

It wasn't until she met Liz that Jan ever felt any attraction to another woman. But their first intimate experience changed Jan forever. It unlocked her soul, she confessed. She was in love with a woman five years her senior.

But Jan rejected Liz frequent requests to move into the large home on Ridgedale Road with her and the girls. Jan was also against any public dining with Liz, except during work hours, usually with other co-workers in attendance. After all, Jan explained, many of her clients were old school. They wouldn't understand their relationship or approve of any hint of the cohabitation of two intimate women. Jan's reputation was too important to jeopardize in any way. Must keep up appearances.

"Who else did you get cards from," Becky asked.

"Several from people at the downtown office," Michael said. "One is from my brother in Houston. He's going to drive up this weekend. I even got one from Elaine."

Becky pursed her lips. "What did she say?"

"Oh, the usual. So sorry. Get well soon. I feel bad for her, Becky. She tried so hard to be nice to me."

"I know. She was nice to me, too, at least in the

beginning."

"I wish her the best, but as long as she works at that place, I think, she's in for nothing but disappointment.

"I never should have been in there," Becky said. "I'm out now, and I'll never go back."

"Neither will I. Promise. It was a weak point in my life. But that's all over now," Michael said.

Becky released his hand and once again gazed into Michael's eyes to glimpse the affection and caring she saw there. "It's a new beginning."

ABOUT THE AUTHOR

Clifford Morris was born and raised in Southwest Kansas. He served with the U.S. Army in Vietnam. During a forty-year career as a salesman, at one time or another, he promoted almost everything under the sun. A long-time sports official and private pilot, he now spends his time playing the piano and writing fiction. He currently lives in Oklahoma.